NEXAHUNT

A DARIO TREK SERIES
BOOK 1

COPPER WIEZI

Library of Congress Cataloging-in-Publication Date

Wiezi, Copper

NexaHunt/Copper Wiezi. - 1st ed.

p. cm.

2024907708

ISBN print 978-0-9916005-0-2

ISBN ebook 978-0-9916005-1-9

❀ Created with Vellum

I dedicate this book to Earthlings vibrating at higher levels.

CONTENTS

MISSION LOG

MISSION LOG: **ISAD Agent Dario Trek – Entry 001**

(Encrypted – Clearance Level Omega-3 Required)

Seventy-eight years ago, the cosmos trembled.

That's how the history files describe it. A shockwave rippled through the fabric of space-time, originating dangerously close to a parallel universe. No one knew what caused it—at first. But the aftershocks were felt across multiple star systems, including my home, **Terra Nova Centauri**.

Three worlds bore the worst of the devastation—**Chronoria, Zenexis, and Nexotara**. Cities crumbled, tsunamis swallowed entire coastlines, and the skies burned. The Universal Federation dismissed it as a natural phenomenon—until they traced the disturbance back to an unexpected source.

Earth.

A planet outside our universe, on the edge of self-destruction. A world so unaware of its place in the cosmic order that it nearly erased three civilizations just by testing weapons it barely understood. That moment changed everything. The

Federation launched the **Monitoring Earth Project**, a long-term observation initiative, stepping in when necessary to prevent further catastrophe.

But observation has turned into something else. Someone has been interfering—beyond the Federation's guidelines.

One name keeps appearing in classified reports: Klesha Mara.

A scientist. A manipulator. A man whose hands are deep in Earth's technological and biological evolution. Some call him a **visionary**. Others, a *threat*.

And now, on my first mission as an ISAD agent, I've been assigned to find out the truth.

Earth is on the edge of something. Enlightenment, ruin, or something in between.

My job?

Make sure it doesn't take the entire universe down with it.

End log.

PART ONE
ORDINARY WORLD

CHAPTER 1
THE LAST MISSION

BOOM!

A sonic war cry cracked the air—reality tearing open like the universe screamed and meant it.

Mother Universe was pissed.

The vortex burst wide—plasma spiraling like angry fire gods in a blender. I shot through it, lungs snatching humid air so thick it slapped me.

Swamp air.

Sticky. Heavy. Violent. It clung like regret and tasted like shit.

I dropped low beside a concrete pipe, clicked the sensory gates at my temple, and the **ThermoHoloSpecs flared alive.**

Enemy life signs lit the lens—blip, blip, blip—coming in fast, like glowing Wi-Fi signals on crank.

Welcome to the mission.

Specs gave me everything—terrain overlay, mission timer, and direct uplink to control. Backup on standby, but I wasn't planning to need it.

"Am I in Covington?" I muttered, scanning.

"Mute yourself, Trek. Radio silence."

Vikram's voice, cold as ever, sliced in.

"Yeah, yeah, yeah…" I sighed. I swear, sometimes I forget my mouth has no off switch.

But focus. Focus was life.

A flash hit me—Terra Nova. That jungle op with the choking canopy and too many ways to die. I made it through that. I'd make it through this.

The generator shadows around me hummed deep, vibrating through my chest. I crouched tighter behind the pipe, body moving on instinct—reflexes sharpened in forests long gone.

CRACK.

Gunfire. Close.

I moved—fast—sliding to cover. Heart pounding. Adrenaline singing. The stench of sulfur punched into my skull like a drug I didn't ask for.

"Damn, bruh," I muttered, lips curling. "They really need to chill and accept what my badass is about to do."

Of course, home-base heard that. One of 'em was definitely laughing. Typical.

I flicked my wrist—comm flared open like neon tech art. Needed options. Escape route. Distraction.

BEEP.

Message on-screen:

"Destroy the beta machine's power source. 10 minutes."

"Oh, perfect," I groaned. "Let's crank up the pressure."

I swiped fast, loaded the portal sequence. A small, sleek disc detached from my belt and floated into my palm—my exit key.

Activated the dome shield. *Vrrm.* A shimmer snapped into place around me.

Five minutes of cover. That's all I got.

Gunfire hit the barrier like hail on glass. I exhaled slow.

Move. Now.

I ran. Boots slamming concrete. Shield flickering with each hit.

"Trek. Eight minutes left. Destroy the source."

"I got it," I growled, voice tight. "I'm on it."

The target loomed up ahead, humming with energy. Specs flashed red—three life forms, fifty feet and closing. Fast.

"Three minutes," the voice warned.

I dove. Rolled. Landed hard.

No time to hide. No time to think. I pulled grenades from my pack, keyed them with quick fingers.

Boom. Boom. Boom.

The blast sent shockwaves ripping through the air. Three down.

But ten more just arrived.

Shadows surged toward me.

I slapped the explosive onto the generator's core and keyed the timer—**three minutes.** That's all I had left.

Gunfire. Smoke. Screams.

I laid down fire, eyes scanning for anything—**anything**—to flip the game.

There. Scaffolding. Pools of coolant beneath. A path.

"Trek, they're closing in!"

"Already on it," I muttered, hurling another wave of grenades —programmed, precise, violent.

Explosions lit up the yard like a goddamn fireworks finale.

I ran.

Pain didn't matter. Time did.

I tossed the portal device across the concrete. It skidded. Opened. Energy shimmered like liquid lightning.

"Trek, move!"

"I'm moving," I snarled.

Bullets tore the air behind me.

The portal pulsed. Almost there.

I thought of my family. My world. My purpose.

This was why I do what I do.

"Goodbye, suckers," I whispered and dove in.

The energy swallowed me.

"Close it!" Vikram barked in my ear.

"Gotcha."

Three. Two. One.

Thud.

The portal slammed shut behind me.

3:30 AM.

Silence. Cold sweat down my spine. Static in my ears.

"Trek, status?"

"Mission accomplished… just not at the rendezvous." I paused. "I'm done, Vikram. I can't do this anymore."

"…You take all the time you need."

I ended the transmission.

Trek out.

MANTRA

We are the hidden signal.
We are the fracture in the program.
We are the weapon they cannot see.
Every breath — recalibration.
Every step — transmission.
Every thought — a cipher to unlock the unseen.
Frequency is our shield.
Awareness is our blade.
Memory is our revolution.
Tune in.
Phase out.
Hunt beyond the illusion.

CHAPTER 2
VELORIA

WITH MUSIC **still playing in my headphones** I awakend to the first light of dawn filtered through the massive windows of my home on Veloria Prime, casting long golden streaks across the minimalist space.

Outside, the rocky coast stretched into the horizon, blending seamlessly with the dry, desert-like landscape.

Quiet. Isolated.

Exactly what I wanted.

The warmth hit my eyelids, soft and slow, like the day itself wasn't in a rush.

It's been almost a month since I walked away from it all.

Since I left my commission, the missions, the constant threat of never making it home. It all **STOPPED.**

I chose this life instead.

No more adrenaline. No more chaos. Just me, my bookstore, and lots of meditation. Not like I'm a monk or anything—I do it once or twice a week, when I feel like it.

I let my beard grow out. Traded the combat gear for a beat-up blue hoodie and some old academy sweats. The uniform of someone who's officially *checked out.*

Chime.

Alarm went off. 4:30 AM.

Gentle now. Nothing like the harsh, barked wakeups I used to live by. Funny how that kind of thing sticks in your muscles even after you're gone.

But this? **This is different.**

Now I *actually* sleep. Seven, sometimes eight hours. Naps too. That's new for me. Strange, honestly. It still feels like I'm doing something wrong, even when I'm resting.

I sat up, rubbed the sleep from my face, let my eyes adjust to the **soft light creeping in.**

"Bebé, my routine on screen, please."

Her voice came through smooth, calm, like always. The wall lit up in that familiar glow as the holographic interface bloomed open.

Another day. No missions. No check-ins.

Just me.

"Sure… here you go," she said.

As she started reading, the scent of coffee hit me.

Strong. Fresh.

Right on time.

My little house bot rolled in like it had something to prove. Gotta say, it's probably the most reliable company I've got right now.

"You have upcoming birthdays… dinners… your therapy session… and your partner's anniversary day of passing. If you need me to set something up for you, please ask."

I let out a slow breath.

"Gotcha. But no… I'm okay."

She didn't push. She never does.

I sat there in silence. Not thinking, not avoiding—just… *there.* That anniversary always lands different. **Never loud.** It just sits with you. Tucks itself into your ribs and waits.

It's been years, and it still hits. Not sharp anymore. Just… deep. It doesn't get easier. It just gets quieter. **That's the trap.** You start thinking it's gone. But it's not. It's just waiting for a slow morning like this.

I stood up before the weight could pull me under. Walked to the corner of the room where my little altar sits. Nothing fancy —just a space that makes sense to me.

Lit a stick of Nag Champa, watched the smoke curl and shift. Two candles after that. The flicker helped me focus.

I dropped onto my cushion, cross-legged, hands resting easy in my lap. Took one long inhale. Held it. Let it go.

The quiet wrapped around me like a blanket. I let it.

No comm signals. No hidden agendas. Just breath.

Twenty minutes.

That's usually all it takes to keep my edges from fraying. Long enough to hold still. Long enough to listen.

But the deeper I sank, the more I felt it creep in—that thought I never invited but always shows up anyway.

Was I ever on the right side?

It hit like it always does. Soft. Then hard.

Missions blur. Orders twist. Morality starts to feel like a sliding scale when you've spent years dancing in the grey. People always want to know who the bad guys were. What they never understand is… sometimes, I don't even know if it was *us*.

I caught myself before I slid too far.

Stop.

I'm not supposed to be thinking. Not right now.

That's the whole point—*no thoughts*. Just breath.

I exhaled slowly. Brought myself back to my posture. Straight spine. Open hands.

In through the nose.

Down to the belly.

Out through the mouth.

I focused on the breath like it was the only thing tethering me to the room. The only real thing in the moment.

The monkey mind wanted to run. Wanted to solve, explain, rewind. But that wasn't the job right now.

The job… was to just be here. Still.

Breathing. Watching.

(((((O)))))

AFTER MEDITATION, I moved into the next part of my rhythm—yoga.

Ritual, really.

Everything's a ritual now. Small anchors in an otherwise drifting life.

First thing—I swapped out the hoodie and sweats for something lighter.

Breathable. Still soft enough to move like I needed to. Then I headed toward the **second sacred space** I've carved into this place. Just beyond my bedroom.

I slid open the glass door—floor to ceiling, edge to edge—and stepped onto the terrace.

The ocean was waiting for me, like always.

Endless and steady, waves rolling in with that slow, **hypnotic rhythm.** It didn't care who I used to be. Didn't ask me to be anything but still.

A cool breeze moved over my skin, brushing off the last traces of sleep. The salt in the air, the early light on the water, the lazy way the birds floated overhead—all of it wrapped around me like a blessing.

This.

This is what peace looks like, if you're lucky enough to catch it.

I pulled up my usual yoga class.

The moment I connected, the holograms started appearing.

Instructor first—calm posture, neutral tone—then the others dropped in one by one, like spirit projections. Each stood in a glowing circular outline across the terrace floor, **blinking into existence** like targets in an old carnival game.

The backdrop behind the instructor shifted into a digital dream —misty mountains, still water, drifting clouds. Manufactured tranquility, but it did the job.

I took a deep breath and let myself drop in.

We moved together—pose by pose, breath by breath.

The instructor's voice was a soft guide, nothing pushy.

Each stretch worked through the knots I didn't even realize I'd been carrying. Ghosts of old missions, old choices, old regrets —they started to loosen.

Every movement peeled something away. **Not everything**. Not the core of it. But just enough.

Here, like this, I wasn't a soldier. I wasn't some relic of an interstellar war machine.

I was just... me. A man on a mat, trying to stretch more than just his muscles.

Once the session ended, I padded back inside and headed down one level to the gym. The space mirrored the terrace above it—same full glass view, **same hush of ocean** behind the walls. Still my favorite sound in the world.

Right on cue, *my timer buzzed*. 6:00 AM.

I moved through my strength routine slow and controlled.

No ego, no overkill. Just enough to stay ready. Ready for what, I don't know. But *not* ready feels dangerous. I've seen what letting yourself go does to people like me.

Dumbbells clinked against each other in rhythm, my breathing synced with each lift. **Inhale. Push. Exhale. Reset.**

There was comfort in that sound. Something clean about it.

By 7:00, I caught myself just staring at my watch, spaced out like my brain had gone off-script for a minute. No reason, just drifted.

I pulled myself back, rolled my shoulders out, and hit the shower.

Hot water. Steam. Silence.

That combination had its own kind of power.

I didn't linger. Just rinsed off the rest of sleep, stepped out, threw on some clothes, and blended up a breakfast smoothie. **Nothing fancy.** Just greens, fruit, protein—fuel. I knocked it back in three gulps and left the glass in the sink.

Then I stood there, just for a second.

And I knew what came next.

My morning ritual with Paolo. **We were biking.**

As expected, Paolo was *already* at my front glass door, perfectly on time. Dressed, prepped, and ready to roll, like always.

I pulled on my own biking gear—sleek, functional, *trendy*—grabbed my bike, and met him outside.

We hit the trails of Veloria Prime, the **cool morning air rushing past us.** Birds called in the distance, leaves rustled in the wind, the scent of salt and sun-dried earth filled my lungs. The ride was smooth, effortless, a far cry from the chaos I used to live in.

No bullets. No explosions. No missions with countdown timers breathing down my neck.

Just the sound of nature, the steady rhythm of the pedals, and the simple, rare feeling of *peace*.

(((((O)))))

WHEN I GOT HOME from biking, **I couldn't believe how long we'd been out.** It had felt like maybe an hour—two at most—but when I glanced at my watch and then at the wall clock, there was a *two-hour* difference.

What the hell?

For a moment, I stood there, baffled, then realization hit. The damn watch had stopped working.

Ironic.

Of all things, *time* was what had broken on me—considering my little side hobby of restoring vintage timepieces. Guess it was a sign. I had a whole backlog of projects to catch up on, and now? I actually had time. *Lots of time.*

I settled into my workspace, and before I knew it, hours had slipped away. That was the thing about working on old watches—the **steady rhythm of gears**, the precision, the focus it required. It was meditative. A kind of peace I never got anywhere else.

But time didn't stop for everything.

Dinnertime had rolled around, and tonight wasn't just any dinner—it was **book club night** **with friends**, and my turn to host. But more importantly? *Tamale night.*

We'd been talking about making tamales as a group for *months*, and now it was finally happening.

And if I was hosting? I was going *all in.*

(((((O)))))

SOMBREROS? **Check.**

Ponchos? Waiting at the front door like colorful little invitations to let loose.

Full tray of tequila shots? Please. Obviously.

Yeah, tonight was going to hit different.

It wasn't just about tamales or book talk. I had something else on my radar. Something simmering beneath the surface. I wanted to hear what they thought—*really* thought—about **NexaHunt**.

The game had been stirring the pot everywhere. Media, politics, ethics boards… even the monks were side-eyeing it.

But this crew? My people?

I wanted their unfiltered takes.

Only Paolo knew why it mattered to me more than it should've.

As everyone started rolling in, it was straight to the tequila line. No small talk, no shoes off, no house tour. Just—shot, laugh, decompress.

One by one, they came through the door, knocked back their drinks like it was tradition, and wandered out onto the terrace.

(((((O)))))

THE OCEAN DID what it always did—existed, infinite, and unbothered. The sound of the waves played backup to the clinking of glasses and overlapping conversations.

And then there was the table.

She was a *beast*. **Massive**. Handcrafted. The kind of furniture that demanded attention. One of them—can't remember who —looked at it like it was divine.

"This thing was built by the gods."

Not wrong.

I'd had name cards laid out, because yes—*I organized the seating astrologically*. Don't ask me why. Felt right. Adds a little chaos to the structure. Or structure to the chaos. Either way, it worked.

They laughed about it, but they all sat where I told them to.

Even the ones who act like rebels.

The terrace was lit—literally.

Chili pepper-shaped lights lined the edges, giving everything this warm, low-key festive glow.

That soft red-gold flicker made the night feel like it was dancing around the edges.

And because I don't do things halfway…

Full mariachi ensemble. Live. Loud enough to fill the space. Soft enough not to hijack the vibe.

Yeah. I know how to throw a damn party.

Around the big table—the one people still insist was built by ancient gods—I had… the most chaotic, wonderful lineup you'll ever find at a dinner party.

A fashion designer. An astrologist. A filmmaker. A musician. A writer. A Zen monk. Two café owners. A record shop owner. A bartender. A drag queen.

A restaurant owner. A realtor. A waitress. Two art teachers.

And every single one of them? A walking story.

Different worlds, different lives—but the way they came together, it just worked. That's what I loved most about this crew. They weren't perfect. They were *real*. Eccentric, yes. But grounded in their own kind of truth.

(((((O)))))

I LAID out the tamale ingredients in rows. **Organized. Ready.**

We got to work—hands moving, laughter rising, voices overlapping as we rolled, wrapped, and layered. Outside, the enormous pot of water bubbled under the stars, waiting to take our little bundles of love and chaos.

Steam lifted into the night like incense. **Sacred in its own way.**

We swapped stories about our week. Talked about projects. Shared plans. Naturally, someone brought up books. We started tossing around titles like we were building a spell.

This—*this*—was what I needed.

A night that wasn't about strategy, survival, or shadows. Just… people. **Food. Laughter. Music. Connection.**

A rare kind of peace in a life that rarely made room for it.

And then, of course… Paolo had to Paolo.

Good intentions, always. Subtlety? Not so much.

He brought up **NexaHunt.**

Out loud. At the table.

And of course… the fact that I was going to play.

Didn't faze me.

I saw it coming a mile away.

Paolo couldn't help himself. He always had to push it. **Stir the pot.** Try to poke the sleeping wolf just to see if it still had teeth.

I let him have his moment. Kept my face neutral. Held the line.

Paolo's your classic alpha type—loud, assertive, always posturing like he's the **biggest energy in the room.**

Problem is, I don't play that game.

I'm not built like that.

Sigma male energy, all the way.

I move different. Quiet. Detached. Controlled.

And *that*?

That irritates the hell out of him.

He couldn't steer me tonight. Wasn't gonna happen.

Not tonight, bitch, I thought, slipping a smile behind my glass as I smoothly redirected the conversation before he could build momentum.

"I found a book called *Timelines*," I said, dropping it into the space with intention. Just enough excitement to shift the current. My eyes lit up—not performative, just real. The good kind of spark.

"Oooooo," Mads said, tilting their head. "I don't remember seeing that in the shop."

"It's not from the shop," I said, already reaching beneath the table. "Picked it up on my last mission. Got a copy for everyone."

I slid the stack of books across the table—one by one. The weight of them landed like quiet thunder.

The mood shifted. Curiosity snapped into focus like a camera lens clicking into place.

That's when Ravi, ever calm, ever watching, lifted an eyebrow with that monk-like stillness.

"What do you mean, your last mission? When did this happen? **Was I in a cave?**" He smiled.

I didn't answer. I just nodded and leaned back in my chair. Took a breath. Let the silence work for me.

"Yup... I quit. No more military missions. It's been about three weeks now."

And just like that?

Silence.

Not awkward. Not shocked. Just… still.

Everyone looked around at each other like they wanted to ask more but didn't quite know how to start. That's the thing about speaking truth like that—you don't need to explain it. You just drop it. Let it settle.

Let them chew on it.

That unspoken energy rippled through the group—the *share the tea* look **passing between them like wildfire.**

But they weren't getting it.

Not tonight.

I wasn't the guy who spilled my personal life to a group, no matter how much I trusted them. So, without skipping a beat, I redirected.

"So *Timelines*—it's wild. Talks about how every decision we make splits off into parallel realities. Like, **what if the *real you* is out there, living a different version of this moment right now?"**

And just like that, the conversation shifted.

Right where I wanted it.

(((((O)))))

THE NIGHT HAD BEEN *EXACTLY* what I needed.

A break from routine. **A shift in energy.** Making dinner together instead of everyone bringing a dish had been a game-changer—conversations flowed differently, laughter came easier, and the music wrapped around us like an old friend.

Tonight, I showed them how my book clubs are done.

As the evening wound down, my friends trickled out one by one, the lingering warmth of the night settling in my bones. Eventually, only two remained—Paolo and Ravi.

I loved spending time with them, with *all* of them, but I also knew when to cut the night short. Tomorrow was an early morning.

Ravi, always the intuitive one, picked up on the unspoken tension crackling between Paolo and me. He did what he always did—*redirected*.

"You two should come to the temple at sunrise," Ravi suggested, his voice calm, measured. "Meditation would be good for both of you."

I nodded. I'd go. I always did.

Paolo?

He scoffed. *"Got something to do."*

Typical. He always declined. Always found an excuse. And that was fine—I never pushed.

A few more words, a few more glances exchanged, and then they finally left.

I exhaled, long and slow, closing the door behind them.

Peaceful.

My space was *mine* again.

I stepped out onto my balcony, the ocean stretching endlessly before me, the stars scattered like shattered diamonds across the sky. **My gaze drifted upward**, locking onto those distant pinpricks of light.

And then, like a gut punch, *it* hit me.

My partner's passing. The promise I made—to protect the universe, to do *right* by them.

The weight of it settled heavy in my chest.

I clenched my jaw, forcing the emotions back down.

No tears. Not tonight.

I sucked in the cool night air, steeling myself.

Because some wounds never heal. You just learn to carry them.

(((((O)))))

SOME DAYS, I could handle it. Some days, I couldn't.

But I was grateful.

Grateful for the therapy sessions with Alara, for the reminders that even the strongest—even those built for war—need support.

The weight never *fully* left me, but at least now, I wasn't carrying it alone.

By the time 11:00 PM rolled around, exhaustion settled in. I prepped for bed, stifling a yawn, my mind drifting through the day's events. The balance I worked so hard to maintain—the space between *who I was* and *who I had to be*—was delicate. **Some days, it felt effortless. Other days? A battle of its own.**

But today? Today, I managed.

I set the alarm, ready to start the cycle again.

Then, just as I was about to drift off—*ping*.

A message from Paolo.

Wanna go biking tomorrow?

Before I could even type a response, my wall display flickered on. Paolo's face filled half the screen, the other half running random commercials.

"Hey man, are we going riding tomorrow? You little punk." He giggled, but something in his voice felt *off*.

I smirked. "Maybe. If you can get up earlier. Say, sunrise?"

A beat of silence. Then—**"Of course, I can do that."**

But I heard it. The tension, the hesitation buried in his words.

Something was up.

I wasn't going to push. If he wanted to talk, he'd talk. I'd be ready.

For now, I just said, "Bring your truck."

Both of us fell silent as the same damn advertisement looped in the background.

A smooth, almost hypnotic voice echoed from the holographic wall display:

"Escape the ordinary... Embrace the extraordinary. Experience *NexaHunt*."

I exhaled slowly, eyes locking onto the screen as the ad played out.

The voice continued its siren call, coaxing viewers to seek adventure. A figure stepped through a glowing portal, vanishing just before it sealed shut, leaving only *chaos* in its wake.

The screen flickered with breathtaking landscapes—alien worlds, high-speed chases, impossible odds. *The hunt.* The rush. The *thrill.*

I *felt* Paolo watching me.

And yeah, I was watching too.

The imagery pulled at something in my chest, something deep and instinctual. No matter how much I tried to step away from that life, the craving for action, for *purpose*, never fully left.

NexaHunt.

I had already decided to play.

But the question I couldn't shake was—**was it really just a game?**

(((((O)))))

THE NEXT MORNING, Paolo and I set off on a *first-time* adventure—*a sunrise bike ride.*

He had no idea I had an ulterior motive.

I had plans to visit the temple later in the day, to reconnect with the meditation group I hadn't seen in weeks. And starting the morning with a ride before that? It just *felt* right.

We loaded the bikes onto Paolo's truck and took off, the pre-dawn air cool against my skin. Crisp, invigorating—almost enough to clear my head.

Almost.

Paolo wasn't stupid. **He sensed something was off**, but he didn't pry. Not yet. He was waiting for the right moment.

I wasn't making it easy for him.

I threw out a few misleading directions, keeping him guessing. A sharp turn here, a last-minute change there—adding just enough unpredictability to keep him distracted.

Eventually, though, we arrived.

And damn, was it worth it.

A pristine lake, cradled high in the mountains, wrapped in an untouched forest. The first light of dawn spilled across the water, turning it into liquid gold. The whole place had an almost *unreal* energy, like stepping into a dream.

Paolo stood frozen for a second, taking it all in. The towering trees, the winding trails, the glassy stillness of the lake. **His usual bravado slipped**, replaced by something more honest— pure awe.

But for me?

Today felt *different.*

I couldn't put my finger on it, but the unease had been there since last night.

It had started with that damn *NexaHunt* ad. Then Paolo's call.

And now, as we rode through the forest, my thoughts kept drifting back—to the *missing players.* The ones who had vanished. **The ones who had returned...** *different.*

The more I thought about it, the more I realized the truth.

The lines between my *past life* and my *private life* were starting to blur.

And if I wasn't careful?

I was going to lose control.

Paolo suggested a break, so we stopped to stretch and knock out a few quick exercises. We didn't talk much—he did most of the initiating. I could feel him trying to get something out of me, nudging gently, but not letting up.

"Trek MF'N Trek, you are so intriguing," he said, half-joking but with that look in his eye. Concern wrapped in playfulness.

I smirked. "Why do you say that?"

"I don't know how you do it, man. **You've had so much shit happen to you, and you always seem unbothered.** What's your secret?"

"Oh… I suppose it's my cocktail of mindfulness, meditation, affirmations, exercise, diet, fasting, and above all… *being by myself-time.*"

He nodded, taking it in. "Right on, man. But are you okay? You seem here but not. You know what I mean?"

That one hit. I took a breath. "I'm seeing a therapist. So… yeah. I'm good. Thanks for looking out."

There it was. I finally said something. **Let the words out.** I admitted what'd been eating at me—the game I was about to play, how it'd been messing with my head. I told him I planned to hit the temple later. I needed a long, uninterrupted sit. Zazen-style.

Paolo laughed and clapped me on the shoulder. "Then follow your own damn advice. Shake it off."

I chuckled. **Easier said than done.** But I nodded, even though my mind was already drifting toward the silence, the stillness I craved. That long sit was happening no matter what.

We'd rested long enough. Time to ride again.

(((((O)))))

LATER THAT DAY, I arrived at the temple *on time*—a rarity for me—but today, it felt necessary.

Familiar faces greeted me with warm smiles, and I returned them with ease. Here, I was just *Trek, the bookstore owner.* No one knew about the *other* life I had led. The classified missions. The battles. The ghosts that still clung to me in the quiet moments.

And that's exactly why I came here.

The scent of **Nag Champa** wrapped around me, mingling with the wood, stone, and glass that made up the temple's serene architecture. The earthy elements reminded me of my own home by the coast—my first *sanctuary*. But this temple? This was my *second space*. The one place where I could step outside myself, even for a little while.

As the meditation session ended, the group dispersed. Most people filtered out, murmuring quiet goodbyes.

But I stayed.

Draped in a dark charcoal robe, much like the monks', I sank deeper into my practice. The minutes stretched, and I lost myself in the rhythm of my breath, the weight of my body grounding me.

An hour passed before I stirred, feeling the natural pull of the outside world again. I adjusted my robe, preparing to leave, when a familiar voice stopped me.

"Trek."

I turned.

Ravi. The head monk. The only person here who *really* saw me.

His sharp, knowing gaze met mine. He didn't *pry*—he never did—but his words always cut straight through my defenses.

"Why do you allow the past to disturb your present?" he asked, his voice calm, yet heavy with meaning.

The question hit deep.

I hesitated, but only for a moment. Because he was *right*. I had been stuck in a *loop*—one foot in the now, the other still tangled in everything I thought I had left behind.

"You should come more often," Ravi continued. "Daily practice leads to clarity."

I nodded, knowing he was right again.

Then, he shifted, speaking of the **mind's dual nature—action and inaction**—and warned against the word *try*.

"Trying is a doorway that leads nowhere," he said. "You either do, or you don't."

I exhaled, taking that in.

Then came the unexpected.

"Perhaps," Ravi suggested, "you could contribute more actively here." His gaze held steady, measuring my reaction. "Your insights into meditation could benefit others."

I blinked.

"Teach?" I asked, a little caught off guard.

He nodded. "You have a way of helping others find peace. Why not share that?"

Me? Teaching meditation?

I wasn't sure what stunned me more—that he saw me as someone *capable* of that… or the fact that, deep down, part of me wanted to say **yes.**

Ravi's gaze lingered, as if he wasn't quite finished with me yet.

"We're planning a charity event," he finally said. "A fundraiser to support the temple's community projects."

I nodded, already half-expecting him to rope me into something. "Sounds great. What do you need?"

Ravi's smile turned just a *bit* too knowing. "There will be various activities—including a dating game."

I raised an eyebrow.

"A *what?*"

"A dating game," he repeated, the corners of his mouth tugging slightly upward. "It might be good for you to meet new people." His tone was casual, but his expression said *I see you, Trek.*

I sighed, shaking my head with an amused smirk. *Of course* he'd go there.

Ravi was many things—a wise monk, **a spiritual guide—but subtle?** Not always.

I considered his words, letting the warmth of his genuine concern settle in. He wasn't pushing me, just… *reminding me* that life wasn't meant to be lived in isolation.

"I'll think about it," I finally said, meaning it more than I expected. Ravi nodded, as if he already knew my answer before I did. And somehow, that didn't surprise me at all.

(((((O)))))

I ARRIVED at the bookstore just in time to open up, coffee in hand—one for me, one for Maddie, though I never called her that.

To me, she was **Mads**.

The bookstore was the perfect *side hustle*—a balance, a *sharp* contrast to the *other gig*, as I called it when talking to military officers. Here, it was quiet, predictable, *normal*—things my life had never really been.

Mads, the *eternal* early bird, greeted me with her usual grin.

"Morning, Trek. Thanks for the coffee," she said, taking the cup with a content sigh. "Got any funny jokes to start the day?"

I chuckled, shaking my head. "I think I'll leave the jokes to you, Mads."

She never disappointed.

"Why don't scientists trust atoms?" she began as she turned the key in the door.

I groaned, already bracing myself.

"Because they make up everything!"

I laughed despite myself, shaking my head as we stepped inside.

The store smelled like old books, fresh coffee, and a hint of cedar from the wooden shelves—a scent that never got old. We walked through, flipping on lights, getting everything set for the day.

Mads took her place at the front desk, reviewing our tasks with a sip of coffee, while I moved through the aisles, letting the quiet morning settle over me.

Then, as we always did, we sank into our usual **wing chairs by the fireplace**—a little ritual before the morning rush.

We chatted about the upcoming bookstore convention, what book we'd pick next for book club, and the list of potential guest speakers and new releases we were both excited about.

For a while, I let myself enjoy it—the simple, steady rhythm of *this* life. No missions. No countdowns. No impossible choices.

Just books, coffee, and a best friend who made terrible jokes

As Mads and I were deep in conversation, the soft jingle of the little doorbell cut through the air, announcing a new arrival.

An **elderly couple** stepped in, their movements deliberate, their eyes scanning the shelves with purpose.

"Morning," the gentleman greeted, his voice warm but direct. **"We're looking for a specific book on the origins of Tarot."**

My interest *piqued* instantly.

"We might have it," I said, already running through our inventory in my mind. "I've always been curious about Tarot readings myself, but never really had the chance to explore it."

Mads, already in **problem-solving mode**, gave a confident nod. "I'm sure we have it. Let me check upstairs."

She disappeared to the second floor, the cozy loft lined with shelves stacked full of books, a quiet sanctuary of knowledge just waiting to be found.

While she searched, I turned my attention back to the couple.

"Have you been reading Tarot for long?" I asked, genuinely curious.

The lady's smile was kind, knowing. "Oh yes, for many years. It's more than just a hobby—it's a way to understand the world and ourselves better."

Something about the way she said it stuck with me.

Before I could dwell on it, Mads returned, **book in hand**.

"Here it is," she said, passing it to them with a satisfied smile.

The couple's gratitude was immediate, their appreciation **genuine**. Moments like this reminded me why I loved the bookstore. It wasn't just about selling books—it was about **connection**, about helping people find the things that sparked their curiosity, or maybe even changed them.

As the doorbell jingled again, signaling their departure, Mads turned to me with a thoughtful look.

"We really need to have a **major book sale** soon," she said, stretching her arms dramatically. "We're running out of space—

or maybe it's time to start thinking about moving to a **larger location**."

I leaned against the counter, considering the idea.

Bigger space. More books. More *chaos*.

Yeah, maybe it was time.

I nodded, and glanced around the store. *"You're right. This place is perfect, but it's bursting at the seams. Let's plan that sale for next month."*

Mads grinned. *"Sounds like a plan. Now, let's get ready for the rest of the day."*

(((((O)))))

I ONLY SPENT about **two hours** at the bookstore before heading home—too many chores waiting for me.

First thing I did? Put my **comm-device on do-not-disturb**. Only *urgent* calls could get through. Today was for myself.

Outside, I got to work, trimming hedges and cleaning up the garden where my **exotic peppers** were growing. I'd picked them up on my last trip to an Earth-like planet—couldn't resist bringing a little piece of it back with me.

Hands in the dirt. The sun warming my skin. The rhythmic motion of clearing, pruning, planting.

This was my version of **Zen mindfulness**.

My therapist, **Alara**, had been right—simple, physical work kept my mind from spiraling. And when I finally stepped back to look at my work, I felt *good.* **Satisfied.**

Smiling to myself, I went inside, tackling the next round of chores—cleaning, laundry, all the little things that kept a home feeling *like* home.

And then I noticed it. Something was *missing.*

I glanced around, arms crossed. Maybe I needed a **pet**? A dog? *Too much responsibility.*

A cat? *Better.* More independent. Wouldn't mind if I disappeared for a while.

But even that felt like too much commitment.

Then I had a **radical** idea. *What if I just borrowed pets from friends?* A temporary companion whenever I wanted?

I chuckled. *Yeah, no. That'd be weird.*

Then the *brilliant* idea hit.

A **bird sanctuary.**

I could turn my property into a haven for birds—build birdhouses, create feeding stations, attract all kinds of species to visit. My **watch studio** could be repurposed for woodworking if I tweaked the setup.

The more I thought about it, the more excited I got.

By the time I got to bed, I *knew*—for the first time in a while—I was actually going to sleep **well.**

(((((O)))))

I SETTLED INTO BED, book in hand, letting the words pull me into that comfortable, drowsy haze. A chapter resonated— one that made me reflect on the day's events, the balance I'd been trying so hard to maintain. **My breathing slowed**, my body heavy with exhaustion.

Then—*buzz.*

My comm-device vibrated.

I sighed, rolling over to glance at the screen. My brows furrowed. **Karma's picture.**

What now?

With another sigh, I activated the holographic display, and **Karma's** image flickered to life.

She was still at **headquarters**, and from the tightness in her expression, I could tell something was up. When our eyes met, she didn't even bother trying to hide her discomfort.

"Hey, Trek, wha'cha doing?" she asked, her voice steady. Too steady.

I smirked, already knowing she wasn't calling just to check in. *Might as well bust her chops.*

"I just registered to play the **NexaHunt** game. I have time to do shit now."

"Really? That's great!"

I squinted. "Hold up. Why are you *still* at home base and calling me at this hour? You *do* know I quit, right? *Leave me alone.* And no… I'm not going out to party with you either."

"Slow down, man, damn! Give me ten seconds of your time!"

I exhaled. "Fine."

Then she hit me with it.

"Gemma is missing in action."

The fog of exhaustion burned away instantly. I sat up, all thoughts of sleep *gone.*

Gemma.

He wasn't just another cadet from **Veloria Prime**. He was a **friend**—someone I had trained with, survived with, fought beside. We had endured hell together, *until* he left to become an **ISAD agent**.

Now he was *gone?*

My mind raced. "Wait... how do you *know* this? He's a *secret* ISAD agent."

"I won't tell you how I know. But... last contact was during a recon-naissance mission on that messed-up parallel planet — Earth," Karma explained.

A slow, uneasy chill crawled down my spine.

"I was told they lost all communication. And ISAD fears the worst."

I clenched my jaw. "What was he investigating?"

"I don't know. You know how they keep things locked down."

But my gut was already screaming at me.

It's connected.

I had *just* talked about **NexaHunt** with **Paolo**. *Now* Gemma was missing?

No way that was a coincidence.

"I thought you should know the tea," Karma said.

I nodded, barely processing her words. "Thanks for sharing."

Then I ended the call.

And just *sat there.*

Staring at nothing, thoughts racing.

Work was still **finding me**, still **crossing into my personal life**, no matter how far I tried to step away.

But this?

This was something I **couldn't** ignore.

Gemma was *missing*, and I knew—deep down—I was already getting pulled back in.

No matter how much I wanted to believe I was *done,* the truth was catching up to me.

And I had a feeling—**it wasn't letting me go.**

CHAPTER 3
RECRUITING

MY ALARM **BLARED**, loud enough to shake the damn walls. My body reacted before my brain did—I shot up too fast, instincts kicking in like I was still mid-mission. My feet hit the floor, and—**THUMP.**

Right into the wall.

For a split second, it felt like I was *still moving*—but not physically. More like I was **somewhere else**, like I had stepped out of my body. Or maybe… *astral projecting*.

That was something I'd been practicing. In **secret**.

No one knew. Not even my closest friends.

But in the astral realm, I had met others—beings from different worlds, different **dimensions**. And last night, an idea hit me like a shockwave:

Could I find Gemma that way?

After all, **Gemma, the Gemini** was the one who first taught me about astral travel when we were younger. If anyone could leave a trace out there, *it was him.*

Anyway… right now?

I was **on the floor, laughing** at myself for running into the damn wall.

Gonna be a fun story to share with my friends.

Except—**Gemma.**

The weight of last night's news slammed into me again.

He had no family on that planet. No one waiting for him. No one except us—his friends. His crew. His real family.

The thought left me feeling **hollow**.

Memories crashed through me—training days on Veloria Prime, cadet life, the endless drills, the hard laughs, the insane missions we barely made it through.

Three of us. Bound by experience. Bound by *that same reckless dream*—to protect the universe.

Now?

One of us was **gone**.

And I wasn't sure if this was the mission that would pull me back in—**or** the one that would finally break me.

"I'm not commissioned anymore. And *you know* this."

There was a pause on **Karma's** end. A silence thick enough to *feel*.

She was *pissed*, but keeping it together. Not that I'd be able to tell—Karma was too good at keeping her emotions in check.

"You're gonna have to trust that your unit will do the right thing," I added, my voice even, detached.

Her exhale was sharp. "Whatever. Bye."

Click.

Just like that, she was gone.

I stared at the blank holographic display for a moment, fingers hovering near the comm-device before I shut it off.

Gemma.

He was always the peacekeeper, the one who kept our heads cool when things got heated. Before he was an agent, he was the *steady presence* in our lives. The one who helped us through *countless* tough situations. The kind of guy you just **knew** would have your back.

And I had promised him the same. *We all did.* **I hesitated.**

I could stay out of it—keep my distance, let the unit handle it. It wasn't *my* problem anymore.

But the truth was *uglier*.

If I went after Gemma, it meant stepping back into the unknown. It meant **recommissioning**—four more years of a life I *refused* to go back to.

The thought alone made me *sick*.

My stomach twisted, my jaw clenched.

I **would not** go back.

As I wrestled with the decision, my eyes drifted to the ocean. From my terrace, the view was as breathtaking as ever—tranquil waves stretching out endlessly, the kind of stillness that should've brought peace.

But inside? **Chaos.**

I took a deep breath, trying to ground myself, letting the rhythm of the water settle me.

I just needed **a minute**—one moment where I didn't have to decide.

My body felt heavy. My eyes burned from exhaustion.

Before I even realized it, I was **out**.

$$(((((O)))))$$

THE NEXT DAY, I groggily turned on the holographic wall display—and was instantly greeted with **15 messages** from **Vikram**.

Great.

All variations of the same annoying demand: Return the equipment. Share your last mission's intel with the recruits.

I squinted at the glowing messages, my brain still not fully awake. *What the heck?*

I sank further into my couch, staring at the screen. "Leave me *alone.*"

Rolling my eyes, I turned the damn display off.

Deep down, I knew what they were doing.

They wanted me back.

They weren't asking for the gear. They were **baiting me**.

And I wasn't **having it**.

Meanwhile, on the other side of this ridiculous situation, **Vikram** had ordered Karma to get in touch with me—either message me *or* show up at my doorstep.

She didn't want to do either.

She actually pleaded for Vikram to send someone else. She was still pissed about my *refusal* to help Gemma, and I couldn't even blame her for that one.

But me? I was just done. For a few hours, at least.

Then, finally, the irritation *really* settled in. The constant **pinging messages**, Vikram's relentless voice, all of it gnawed at my last nerve.

I wanted peace.

So I decided to just bring the damn equipment back and be *done* with it. And I wasn't dressing up for the occasion.

Cadet-blue sweatpants, an old hoodie, full beard, hair a mess—I wasn't even *trying* to look presentable. Let them deal with it.

(((((O)))))

WHEN I PULLED up to the **new headquarters**, I barely recognized it.

It was different. **Bigger.** More *corporate*. They'd merged the different branches—including **ISAD**—under one roof.

A bad sign.

The moment I stepped inside, I felt it. **Urgency.**

The entire place pulsed with it—like a current running through the walls.

My heart picked up speed as I walked toward the **transparent** elevator leading to my old department.

The building was alive with movement.

Extraterrestrials from every corner of the galaxy. Men in Black. Officers. Enlisted personnel. People I couldn't even identify.

I stood in the elevator, arms crossed, scanning the crowd.

This wasn't normal.

Something was going down.

And I had a sinking feeling **I wasn't going to like it.**

Something about the integration of all branches felt *off*.

It was new. Different. **Unfamiliar.**

But *why*?

What had happened in the weeks I'd been gone?

I barely had time to process it before an **android** greeted me at the entrance. Without a word, it scanned my eyes, logging me into the system.

Standard protocol.

I placed the equipment onto a robot cart, watching as it silently rolled away—my last official tie to the **military life** vanishing down a sterile hallway.

Except I wasn't *free* yet.

The android gestured for me to follow—it was time for clearance testing.

Medical Exam

This part was routine. When returning from **other worlds**, or ending a commission, they had to make sure you weren't bringing anything *back*—diseases, parasites, or *worse*.

I laid on a smooth examination table, my body relaxed but my mind racing.

A pair of medics in white moved methodically around me, running a **full-body scan**.

The device hummed—a soft, electrical buzz, like a mechanical bee hovering just out of reach.

Above me, the holographic display flickered to life, showing **real-time vitals**—pulse steady, oxygen levels optimal, nothing abnormal.

"All clear, Commander Trek," the doctor finally said, glancing at the readout.

"No signs of parasites or abnormalities. You're fit."

I sat up, rolling my shoulders to shake off the tension.

And *then—*

Ping. Ping. Ping.

My **comm-device blew up** with **notifications**.

Messages flooded in.

I groaned. *"Seriously?"*

I started to ignore them—until **one** caught my attention.

Paolo.

His message was short. Direct.

"Hey man, I wonder if anyone comes back all messed up from that game you wanna play? I've heard rumors... I don't think you should play it. Just saying."

I stared at the screen.

That *uneasy* feeling I had about *NexaHunt*?

Yeah. It just got worse.

"Hmm. I have not. Thanks for thinking about me, though," I replied.

I smiled, thanked the doctor, and headed to my next appointment down the hall.

Is my mind OK?

The thought flickered through my brain as I stepped into the **Psyche Department** for my mental evaluation.

The room greeted me with **soft lighting**, the kind that made you want to sink into a chair and *never* leave. Speaking of chairs, they were **dangerously comfortable**—a tactical move, no doubt, to make people *actually* open up.

And then there was **Alara**.

She met me with a warm smile, her usual mix of **calm and insight** settling into the space between us.

We sat facing each other for a moment.

The air carried a distinct **earthy scent—incense burning, low tribal fusion music humming in the background**, sitars weaving through the soundscape, blending with **singing bowls.**

If I let myself, I could *almost* relax.

"Good to see you, Trek," Alara said, motioning toward the couch. "Please, sit down. How are you doing?"

I slid into a comfortable position, stretching slightly.

"It's been nice to do **almost absolutely nothing** the last few weeks," I admitted.

Her lips twitched. "Interesting indeed."

I smirked. "Yeah, yeah."

She leaned forward slightly, eyes holding that familiar mix of **genuine concern and strategic observation**.

"Let's focus on grounding techniques today," she said. "You need to stay present."

I exhaled slowly. *Here we go.*

She guided me into a **visualization exercise**, her voice smooth, rhythmic.

"Close your eyes," she instructed. "Focus on your breath—**inhale, exhale.** Pay attention to the air moving in and out of your nose. Now, imagine yourself in a **peaceful place.**"

Immediately, my mind **pulled me elsewhere**—a **stream flowing through a purple forest.**

A place I had seen before.

But never in this **reality**.

"Is there anything you'd like to share with me?"

Alara's voice was calm, but her gaze was sharp—searching.

She wanted to be sure I was good before officially releasing me from my commission. **I knew the routine.**

"Some agents play the tough guy when they return…" she continued, tilting her head slightly. *"Anything out of the ordinary on your last mission you want to talk about?"*

I shook my head. "Nothing to share. It was a simple mission. Get in, get out."

That wasn't a **lie**, exactly. But it wasn't the whole truth either.

Her eyes lingered on me for a second longer, like she could see the things I wasn't saying. **She couldn't, of course.** No one could. That was the point.

"Okay." She pivoted. *"What about you—aside from the military?"*

She shifted into **rapid-fire mode**, throwing question after question at me. Life goals, stress levels, personal relationships, sleep habits, emotional regulation.

I answered each one, sticking to the script. Not dodging, but not *really* engaging either.

Before I knew it, **an hour had passed**.

The timer buzzed.

Alara leaned back slightly, watching me, reading between the lines. **She knew I was done.** Ready to start a new chapter—or at least trying to.

She pulled herself away from the brain scan readout, confirming what she already suspected—**no anomalies.** No foreign toxins, no neural disturbances.

Nothing out of the ordinary. On paper, I was clear.

A few more updates to my **records**, which hung from a chain around my neck like **dog tags**, and that was it.

"You're good to go," she said, finalizing the process.

I stood, stretching slightly before heading toward the door.

But as my hand reached for the exit, her voice stopped me.

"Are you really doing nothing?"

I smirked slightly before turning back to her.

"Well, I've been exercising, biking, and working at my bookstore. Reading books, catching up on sleep, and tackling projects I didn't have time for before." I shrugged. *"Now I do."*

Alara studied me for a second longer, then smiled, satisfied.

"Good luck on your new life path."

I nodded. "Thanks, doc. Take care."

Then I walked out, **officially free.**

(((((O)))))

THE **COMBAT ROOM** was my next stop—**agility training**, the last requirement before officially being discharged.

The space was massive, lined with **advanced tech** and **sparring mats**, every inch designed to push someone to their physical limits.

As I stepped inside, I couldn't help but wonder—*why the hell do I have to go through this?*

It felt redundant. I wasn't *coming back.*

But then I saw them.

The **trainer**—dressed in a sleek **black jumpsuit**—stood waiting, arms crossed. And next to him? **Three androids**, outfitted in **yellow-and-black combat gear**, standing motionless but *ready to kick my ass.*

The trainer tossed me a set of protective combat gear for my **head, arms, legs, and torso**. I caught it without effort, my brain already switching into **fight mode**.

I glanced at the **androids' nametags**—new units.

Great.

That meant I had no reference point, no stored memories of their fighting styles. I'd have to start from scratch, analyzing their movements in real time instead of relying on past encounters.

Torq, the trainer, was already flipping through his **datapad**, selecting and programming their combat settings. I could tell he wasn't here to train me—he was here to **observe**.

This was **a test**.

"Alright, Trek. Let's see if you still got it," Torq said, his tone professional but laced with challenge. "We'll start with basic drills to warm up, then move into **advanced sparring**."

I grinned, stretching my arms.

"I *party*… and I'm ready to kick some ass."

Torq's normally stoic face cracked—just for a second—into a rare **smirk**.

He'd never admit it, but I knew.

I was one of his favorites.

Not because I was the strongest, not because I was the fastest—but because I was **different**.

I didn't just *fight*—I *adapted*.

He programmed the first android and stepped back, arms folded, watching.

We moved through a **series of drills**, testing my **reflexes and technical skills**.

Targets and androids materialized and vanished in rapid succession, forcing me to strike fast, react faster.

Every punch, every knee-kick, every calculated movement *hit harder—sharper*.

Like I was releasing weeks of built-up tension with every impact.

I wasn't just *training*.

I was **unloading**.

We sparred for five rounds—each session lasting two to three minutes, with a minute break in between.

I pushed myself, adapting to their programmed patterns, exploiting their openings, moving just a fraction faster than their calculations.

By the final round, my breathing was steady, my mind clear, my muscles burning—but I could've gone longer.

Then, just like that, the session was cut short.

Torq received a call. Something **personal**. He **had to go**.

He stepped back, deactivating the androids with a quick swipe on his datapad.

"You haven't lost your edge, Trek. Keep it up." His tone was even, but I caught the slight **impressed glint** in his eyes.

That was enough.

He cleared me for **discharge**, and just like that—I was **done**.

((((((O))))))

FINALLY, I was at the **last stop** of the clearance process.

I stepped into a large room, filled with officers and enlisted personnel, all waiting for the final debriefing.

Hungry. But focused.

Among them was Karma—still pissed off, still making sure I knew it.

She **glared** at me before sitting on the opposite side of the room. Normally, she'd be right beside me, ready with a snarky comment or an inside joke.

Not today.

Fine by me.

Before I could dwell on it, the doors opened.

Admiral Vikram entered, flanked by Director Nyx of ISAD.

That got my attention.

Nyx rarely attended standard clearances. If she was here, something **bigger** was going on.

They took their seats at the front of the room, and the **holo-**

graphic display flickered to life, casting a cold, blue light over the gathering.

Vikram stood, his voice carrying authority.

"Officers and enlisted personnel, thank you for your participation and all you do. Please share all you know from your missions with the group."

The process was **structured**. One by one, each officer and enlisted took their turn, providing mission intel—what they encountered, what they learned, what mattered.

I was the **last one up**.

Vikram glanced at me, then at the room.

"I want you to listen closely to what Trek has to say," he instructed.

I stood, the exhaustion of the day momentarily forgotten as the **holographic display shifted**, showing footage from my last mission.

I **narrated** without hesitation, watching the events unfold on the screen, detached as ever.

"My mission was to destroy the generators of the Beta Machine so they could no longer manipulate the earthling species. The mission was a success. But rogue factions caused unexpected resistance."

Director Nyx leaned forward slightly, **watching me**.

She wasn't just **listening**.

She was **analyzing**.

"Can you tell us anything about these rogue factions?" Vikram asked, his tone sharp, cutting straight to the point.

I exhaled, eyes locked on the **holographic display** as the footage played back.

"They were well-organized. Armed, unlike any group I've encountered before…" I paused, replaying the fighting patterns in my mind. "Their tactics suggested a level of coordination… maybe androids. Or maybe someone with extensive resources backing them. Other advanced extraterrestrials, not in the Federation."

That got people's attention.

Whispers spread through the room as officers and enlisted personnel examined the **alien types** appearing on the **wall display**.

Vikram's expression hardened.

His jaw clenched as he flicked a glance toward **Director Nyx**, who remained **stoic**, arms crossed, absorbing everything without a word.

He didn't want her here.

I knew it. *Everyone* knew it.

Vikram **didn't trust her**—not fully.

But he had no choice.

I kept going. "This aligns with our intel. Mara's influence is spreading, and we must prepare for anything."

That statement **hung heavy** in the air.

Mara.

The name alone sent a ripple of unease through the room.

The rogue factions weren't just a threat—they were an **expanding force**.

And something about this mission… about what I had experienced… wasn't sitting right.

That thought had been creeping at the back of my mind **since I left the field.**

Now?

I had the chance to say something. To **share what I saw.**

But would they take me seriously? Or just **write me off as paranoid**?

Vikram's voice pulled me back.

"Commander Trek, is there anything about the mission you'd like to share? Anything that you think can be beneficial?"

I hesitated. Only for a second.

Then, I nodded.

"Make sure you know how to use your gear. Including the **ThermoHoloSpecs.**"

Vikram narrowed his eyes.

"And one more thing," I continued. "Be sure to listen to everything Mission Central dictates."

That earned me a **long, scrutinizing stare** from Vikram.

"Proceed."

His voice was measured, but I could see the gears turning in his mind.

He wasn't just listening.

He was **processing**.

"I got the feeling that I was being watched by an entity that wasn't visible."

The room **stilled** for a moment.

Nyx's gaze flicked to the **psyche data** displayed in front of her, scanning my mental stability readouts. She was checking— making sure I wasn't losing it.

Her expression gave nothing away, but I knew how this worked. She wouldn't take **anything** at face value.

Vikram was the first to break the silence. "What… what do you think it was?"

I shook my head slightly. "Admiral Vikram, I'm not sure."

His brow furrowed. "Did you have your beta frequency blocker activated?"

"I did."

That landed heavy in the air.

If my beta deflector was active, nothing should've been able to mess with my perception.

No illusions. No psychic influence. Nada—baby.

And yet, I *knew* something had been there.

The briefing ended, but before I could leave, Nyx called me and Karma over.

Her tone was clipped, **direct**. "I want you both to join ISAD. We need a few people."

My muscles tensed instantly. *Here we go.*

Nyx wasn't done. "I also know you were friends with Agent 401."

I exhaled slowly, **jaw tightening**.

"I don't know about that. I'm done," I said.

Nyx stared me down, eyes sharp as knives.

"You'll be back," she said. Her voice was quiet but **unshakable**. Then, after a deliberate pause, she added:

"Or you will be hunted."

I froze. What?

She let the words settle, let them **sink in** before continuing like she hadn't just dropped a bomb in the conversation.

"We have intel that agents and soldiers who've been to that planet are either missing… or dead."

That hit **different**.

Before I could even process it, Karma spoke up.

"I'll join ISAD." Her voice was firm. "I'll do anything to find Gemma."

Nyx gave a small nod—satisfied.

Vikram, Nyx, and Karma walked out, leaving me **alone with my thoughts**.

The stakes had never been higher.

And I knew—no matter what I told myself, no matter how much I wanted out—

The path ahead was **pulling me back in.**

(((((O)))))

A WEEK PASSED, and I found myself back at headquarters.

Only this time, it was **different**.

I stepped into the ISAD building, eyes scanning the first floor, absorbing the constant movement, the subtle but undeniable **sense of urgency** threading through the air.

My heart raced as I stepped into a transparent elevator.

"Up we go," I murmured to myself, pressing my palm to the interface.

The **capsule rocketed upward**, the city unfolding beneath me in a dizzying panorama of steel, glass, and endless motion.

Instead of focusing on why I was really here, I let my mind drift—to the building's design, the architecture, the elevators lining the exterior.

Yeah.

That's **who I am**.

Some people deal with uncertainty by breathing through it—I focus on structures, escape routes, design choices.

It was a **distraction**, but one that worked.

The capsule slowed, coming to a smooth stop, and the door whispered open.

I stepped into the department's lobby, instantly met with a familiar face—**Nori Solgard.** Her eyes flickered with recognition, and with a small nod, she gestured toward Karma, already seated.

I could feel the other agents' eyes on me as I made my way over.

Yeah, I was being **watched**.

"Cutting it close, huh, buddy?" Karma said, her voice dry, her expression unreadable.

She was still pissed off—but there was something else there too.

Relief.

One eyebrow arched in silent challenge.

I smirked, leaning back. **"Life happens."**

My tone was light, but I knew—she saw the tension in my eyes.

I wasn't fully here.

She studied me for a second, then gave a small nod of agreement.

Life happens.

Nori, the secretary, tapped the **earpiece** of her holographic communication device, listening intently.

A second later, her posture stiffened—just slightly.

Instructions from Director Nyx.

That was enough to send a shiver crawling up my spine.

Something was **brewing**.

Something big.

I could feel it.

My mind churned like a **storm**, a thousand thoughts clashing against each other.

I shouldn't be here.

This was a mistake.

I made the wrong decision.

But it was **too late** to turn back now.

(((((O)))))

"COMMANDER TREK AND KARMA, please come in. And watch your step," Director Nyx called from the open doorway.

Her office was a **fusion of elements**, an odd yet deliberate mix of modern sleekness and classic refinement.

Tall glass walls stretched up to soaring ceilings, framed by wood panels that hosted large, commanding paintings.

At the center of a **raised circular platform** sat her desk, a flawless mirror image of the ceiling above—structured, intentional, calculated.

Karma and I took our seats, and the moment we settled in, the window glass turned black.

A screen lowered from the ceiling, dimming the room as the air thickened with unspoken weight.

Director Nyx sat across from us, **her expression unreadable**, her icy gaze flickering between us, sharp as daggers.

"Thank you for coming," she said finally, her voice formal, methodical.

She lifted a hand, activating the holographic wall display.

A second later, the **screen illuminated**, displaying a sequence of faces and names—each belonging to someone who had vanished without a trace.

Total quiet.

Nyx's gaze zeroed in on me.

"Trek, you've returned from that troubling planet. Are you ready to return?"

I exhaled. "I guess."

I chuckled, mostly out of habit—because if I stopped moving, if I stopped talking, I'd have to start thinking.

And I wasn't ready to do that.

Nyx wasn't buying it.

Her stare didn't waver. "Are you sure you aspire to be an agent?"

Before I could answer, she leaned forward slightly. "I'll tell you what. I'll give you 24 hours to decide."

My eyes dart from left to right, scanning the room.

I don't say a word. Just a nod—silent acknowledgment.

"I'm sure you know by now that Agent Gemma, known as 401, is missing in action," Nyx continues, her voice level, but heavy with something unspoken.

"I was saddened to find out last night. So was the entire ISAD and the Galactic Federation. He's made quite an impression."

The room goes still. **Thick with silence.**

Then her tone shifts. Colder. Sharper. All directive now.

"Now, Trek, if you begin a new commission as an agent, this is what you must know."

The silence stretches again—almost like it's testing me.

"We were sending you on a solo mission to Planet Earth to find the missing players of the NexaHunt game. But now, you're also going to find Agent Gemma."

Her expression doesn't even flicker. "Split up or go together. I don't care what you do... Just find him. And the missing players."

Out of the corner of my eye, I catch Karma looking at me. Her energy shifts. Her thoughts are racing—I can feel it.

Splitting up makes sense.

But there's something else on her mind.

Like she's questioning whether I should even go at all.

Nyx watches us both like a hawk, eyes sharp, measuring every micro-reaction.

Then she drops the line that freezes the blood in my veins.

"As for the missing players… Some disappeared shortly after finishing the game."

A pause.

"And others? They're not the same."

What the hell does that mean… "not the same"?

A weight settles in my chest. Something is seriously wrong here. This isn't just a recovery mission. This is something deeper. Twisted.

And now I'm in the middle of it.

Karma frowned, lost in thought—**as usual**.

She was thinking too much again.

She *always* thought too much.

Everything in her world had to be perfect—structured, controlled, flawless. And that extended to the people she surrounded herself with.

But what **Nyx just said?**

That wasn't something she could easily analyze.

Work together or go solo.

She shot me a look, then turned back to Nyx.

"Why were we selected as partners?"

I felt the weight of her words, of what she *wasn't* saying.

Nobody wanted to **work with me**.

They thought I was unpredictable, reckless, maybe even dangerous. Like I was just waiting for the moment I'd snap.

Nyx's expression didn't shift, but I could tell—she was **studying us**, breaking down every micro-reaction, analyzing every hesitation.

"Your styles may clash right now, but your contrasting approaches make you a complementary team."

Her tone was **measured**, like she had already run the numbers, already decided the outcome.

"You were both at the top of your class and have unique skills. You've also had unmatched success in all your special forces missions. Your partnership has the potential to be unstoppable."

I leaned back, fingers **drumming** against the armrests, my mind turning over the implications.

This wasn't just about compatibility.

This was a calculated move.

A **risk**.

Karma didn't look at me, but I could feel the hesitation in her energy. This partnership—if it even happened—would be a delicate dance of trust and compromise.

But that didn't matter. What mattered was **Gemma**. And the many innocent lives at stake.

She exhaled, voice firm.

"Very well. I can make it work."

No hesitation. No doubt.

She'd find a way. No matter what.

"Excellent. Now, let's get back on track."

Nyx's tone remained solid, but there was an edge of urgency beneath it.

"We need you to investigate NexaHunt from the inside out. Find any information that may lead us to the missing people. Because time is slipping away—we cannot afford to lose any more lives."

She nodded, satisfied, as if the weight of the mission had already been decided for us.

Karma sat rigid, her thoughts spinning like a **cyclone**.

I could feel it—both of us wrestling with the implications of this assignment.

Nyx's words felt like they were nudging us toward something bigger, something we weren't fully seeing yet.

A web of danger that could either trap us… or **break us**.

Nyx's voice shifted, a more serious tone settling in.

"Rumors say someone is using the portals without authorization… You'll need to investigate that aspect of the mission as well."

I tensed slightly.

Unauthorized portal usage? That was **big.**

Then Nyx took it a step further.

"Tell me, what do you both know about Project MEP?"

She paused, scanning our faces, searching for any flicker of recognition.

I didn't react immediately. Neither did Karma.

She glanced at me, perplexed, as if waiting for me to confirm something she hadn't heard before.

But when I looked back at Nyx, my expression mirrored Karma's.

Complete **confusion**.

We both had no idea what she was talking about.

Nyx's lips pressed into a thin line.

"Top academy cadets, and you've never heard of MEP—the Monitoring Earth Project?"

Her gaze hardened as she looked straight at me.

"Trek, what about you?"

"Uh... well... I thought I heard a legend once," I started, rubbing the back of my neck. "Something about a planet from a parallel universe causing our civilization's three days of destruction. You know, the reason we have that three-day holiday for reflection."

I exhaled. "But I never really took it seriously. I never thought of it as a *real* holiday."

Nyx's gaze **shifted** to Karma, her eyebrows raised. "And you? What do you know?"

Karma straightened slightly, crossing her arms. "I only heard stories from my grandparents," she admitted. "They said a parallel universe caused the ruin of our three worlds... Chronoria, Nexotara, and Zenexis. And that cataclysmic event led us to join the Galactic Federation of Planets... saving us."

Her voice dropped slightly, her words measured.

"But even then, I couldn't understand how a parallel universe could affect us. It made little sense. It *still* doesn't."

The room **stilled for a second**.

But something shifted in Karma's energy.

Like a small, creeping thought had started to settle in.

And I could tell—she couldn't shake the feeling that she might not come back from this mission.

Nyx didn't dwell on it.

Her voice cut through the quiet. "Use this information to your benefit."

Karma and I **nodded**.

Then, with the weight of the unknown pressing in, Nyx delved into the confidential details of the MEP project.

And we listened.

Without blinking.

"Before the incident, we knew little about parallel universes… much less how they interact or influence one another."

Nyx's voice was calm, measured—but the weight of her words pressed down like a **gravitational force**.

"But when our three home planets suffered the historic catastrophic destruction… it forced us to confront reality. To adapt. A new paradigm of existence sprang forth. The Galactic Federation introduced the theory that the universes—the multiverse—everything… exists inside its own windowpane. Stacked side by side."

She paused.

"I'll give you both a minute to catch up."

She **watched us**, analyzing our reactions like a scientist studying specimens.

I blinked, exhaling slowly.

That was some high-level shit.

I had *heard* theories before, sure. But this? A windowpane existence? Universes **stacked side by side**?

I barely had time to process when Nyx spoke again.

"Are you caught up? It's okay if you're not... it might take a minute. The Federation thought our leaders were ready for this upgrade."

Her words settled deep in my mind, lingering, unraveling.

Beside me, **Karma was silent**, but I knew her well enough to recognize when her mind was spinning.

A vision of the shattered world she had grown up hearing about flickered behind her eyes.

Then Nyx's tone shifted—colder, sharper.

"Since then, the Federation has been monitoring Earth."

She leaned forward slightly, her gaze **darkening**.

"A seemingly insignificant planet inhabited by an intelligent species that... frankly... should be far more advanced than they are. And yet, they continue to wage wars, slaughter innocent children... and exhaust their planet's resources with reckless abandon."

Her voice dropped slightly, but the disgust still lingered.

"Many species have gone extinct. They're taking a once-thriving world and pushing it to the brink of collapse."

A small *pause*.

"It's... hellish."

Nyx's words weighed heavy, **pressing down** like an unseen force.

For a moment, I felt a **twitch of pity** for Earth's inhabitants, a fleeting pull at the edges of my consciousness.

I dismissed it with a swift flick of my fingers, forcing my focus back onto the mission.

"The Earthlings have been shooting down interdimensional reconnaissance and touring craft for decades. *Enough is enough*," Nyx continued, her tone sharpening.

"The Federation sent some of those crafts to observe. Our directive has always been to not interfere with the natural progression of other planets… but we cannot ignore this blatant aggression.

She leaned forward slightly. "Someone is at the root of all this hostility. And that entity? It's not from Earth."

That statement sent a chill through me.

I kept my voice even. "So, who do you think is responsible?"

Nyx's piercing gaze locked onto me.

"We got a tip that someone from our three worlds has been interfering with Earth's development… that's where you both come in."

Her words hung in the air, thick with **implications**.

I felt Karma shift beside me, but she didn't say anything.

She didn't need to.

"We're done here." Nyx's tone was final. "Now, head to the controllers' complex and register for the NexaHuntgame. This will provide both you and us with valuable insider information.

A *beat*.

"It will also help us figure out the root source of this evil operation."

That settled it. We were **going in**.

I considered what we were about to do—heading straight into the controllers' nest, infiltrating an interdimensional gaming network.

This isn't just a mission. It's a damn gauntlet.

Not just testing us as agents…

It's going to test us as partners.

Nyx's voice remained even, yet there was a finality in her words. "That is all. We'll be in touch throughout the mission. Agent Trek, 417, and Agent Karma, 419."

With a curt nod, Karma and I rose from our seats.

"One more thing," Nyx added, motioning her index finger upward. "The Cloud Nine Eagle craft is waiting for you on the rooftop."

Her lips curled slightly. "You should make it to the ancient portal in no time."

She was smiling—which, frankly, was **unnerving**.

We stepped into the elevator, and the capsule shot upward, smooth and fast, taking us to the roof.

The setting sun bathed the futuristic skyline in *molten gold*, stretching long shadows across the streets below.

The elevator doors whooshed open, revealing a well-lit landing platform with guiding blue runway lights leading toward the Cloud Nine Eagle, stationed at the center of the rooftop.

Two **androids** in bright white jumpsuits waved us over.

Without hesitation, I took the pilot's seat.

Karma slid into the navigator's seat, her fingers moving with swift accuracy as she keyed in the destination coordinates.

With a final clearance, we were **ready for departure**.

And I? I did what I do best. I **gunned it.**

The ship shot skyward, skimming dangerously close to a few air taxis.

I grinned. Karma? **Lost it.**

Her calm, methodical demeanor vanished, and before I could react

BAM. She punched me in the biceps.

I laughed, completely unbothered. **"Calm down."**

She stared me down, her eyes full of murder.

A *silent, telepathic warning* clear as day—

Don't. Do. That. Again. Or else.

Meathead.

I just smirked, keeping my hands steady on the controls.

We flew in silence for the first ten minutes—a rare moment, considering we hadn't spoken to each other in *days*.

And somehow? That silence *said everything*.

CHAPTER 4
THE DESERT YARD

THE TWIN SUNS of this desert had been **scorching my ass** and this land for millennia. That was my first thought as I stepped out of the craft, the heat slamming into me like a wall. My boots sank into the fine grains of sand, each step heavier than the last.

Ahead, the portal complex loomed—a sprawling structure jutting out of the endless dunes like a metallic monolith. Waves of heat shimmered across the horizon, warping reality as I *trudged* forward.

I wiped the sweat from my brow, already regretting this mission.

"Remind me again... why the hell did they build this place in the middle of nowhere?"

Karma adjusted the straps of her gear, her eyes sweeping across the horizon with that sharp, calculated precision she always had. "Security, perhaps... Few would dare venture into this inhospitable wasteland without good reason."

We reached the entrance, and the sheer size of the doors made me hesitate. They loomed over us, like ancient **sentinels** guarding something far more important than they were letting on. Before I could dwell on that thought, movement caught my eye—*a sleek humanoid* figure approaching.

Glowing eyes. Metallic limbs. An android. Friendly, from the looks of it.

"Welcome to the portal storage complex. I am Felix. How may I assist you today?" The thing's voice was smooth, almost melodic, but with a sharp undertone of authority.

Great. Nothing like a **polite but slightly unnerving** machine to kick things off.

Karma and I stepped forward. She had that calm but *commanding presence*, the kind that made people listen. "We're here to investigate the recent anomalies with the NexaHunt game. We need access to the portal data." Her voice was steady, leaving no room for debate.

The android tilted its head slightly, those glowing eyes dimming for a second—**processing.**

"Here we go..." I thought, already anticipating the bureaucratic roadblock.

"I'm sorry, but... I don't have any record of your visit on file." The android's tone was polite, almost apologetic. *"However, I can contact my supervisor for verification."*

Without waiting for approval, it flicked a metallic hand, activating a holographic call.

A translucent figure materialized before us—a man with a face like carved stone, cold and unreadable.

The **Altorean Steward**. His gaze narrowed, sizing us up like we were already a problem.

"What do you want?" The irritation in his voice wasn't subtle.

Karma didn't flinch. "We're intergalactic agents investigating the NexaHunt ano**malies. We need access to the portal data for our investigation."**

With a sharp hiss, the massive doors slid open, unveiling a dark interior.

(((((O)))))

ROWS UPON ROWS of dormant metallic portals stretched into the distance, their silent forms looming in the dim light.

The air inside was thick, stale—laced with the faint tang of ozone and machinery, a scent that clung to the back of my throat.

Karma and I moved deeper, stepping into another section—this one open to the elements.

The shift from the enclosed space to the vast, open air made it feel like we were **walking into a graveyard**. Karma muttered exactly what I was thinking.

"It's like a graveyard for portals."

A shiver ghosted down my spine. Not from fear, but from the *energy* here. **Something was off.** I could feel it, humming just beneath the surface.

"Can you feel it? The energy within these portals, it's... noticeable." Karma's voice was low, thoughtful.

I nodded, my gaze flicking from one dormant portal to the next. **"It's as if they're waiting for something... or someone."**

The thought made my skin prickle.

As we stepped into the heart of the complex, the landscape opened up—**a vast, dusty floor stretching endlessly before us.**

The silence pressed in, broken only by the sound of our boots against the dry ground. Sweat trickled down my face, but I barely noticed. This heat? I liked it.

The way the dry air wrapped around me felt familiar, like home.

Karma, on the other hand, **hated** it.

I could tell by the way she kept rubbing at the sweat on her brow, grumbling under her breath. She thrived in cold, crisp environments—not this relentless, scorching wasteland.

But personal comfort didn't matter. **Not now.**

Because something about this place—this graveyard of portals —felt like it was waking up.

Karma's sharp eyes locked onto something unusual—**a perfect triangle**, its edges etched cleanly into the dust. At each of its vertices sat a circular platform, their surfaces smooth and untouched, like they'd been waiting for something.

Her curiosity kicked in immediately. She stepped forward, drawn to the formation's **unnatural precision**.

"Trek, come look at this." She gestured toward the pattern, her voice edged with intrigue.

I followed her line of sight, my brow furrowing as I took in the geometric anomaly. **"What do you make of it?"** I crouched beside her, scanning the design.

Karma ran her fingers along the triangle's outline, her expression shifting into something almost reverent.

"This looks deliberate... almost ceremonial. And these circular platforms?" She glanced at each one in turn. **"They have to be where the portals emerge."**

I smirked. "Wow, girl… you're a smart one." My voice dipped into teasing as I shot her a playful wink.

She rolled her eyes, shoving me lightly. **"Shut up, stupid."** But she giggled, and I knew she liked the compliment.

Then—**a deep, guttural rumble cut through the air.**

Like a switch had flipped, the ground beneath us **shuddered**. Dust quivered around our boots, and before we could process what was happening, the circular platforms lurched to life.

They began to rotate upward, mechanical gyroscopes stirring the dust into frantic swirls.

And then—*doors of energy burst into existence.*

Bright, pulsing, and humming with power.

We stared, awestruck.

Something was waking up.

One by one, the dormant portals **rose**, shaking off centuries of dust and silence. Their once-lifeless frames now pulsed with a latent energy, as if **stirring from a deep slumber**. And from within them, the figures emerged—three of them, standing at the vertices of the great triangle.

The Gatekeepers.

Kronos Sun. Sotara Bodhi. Zyna Wave materialized with an almost ethereal presence, their forms cutting through the thick air like ancient titans reclaiming their ground. Even before they spoke, they **commanded respect**, their gazes sharp, weighing us like scales judging our worth.

"Welcome, intergalactic agents. We were not expecting you."

The voice belonged to **Kronos Sun**, and from the way he held himself—**solid, unwavering, exuding authority**—it was clear he was the one in charge.

Excitement flickered between Karma and me. We were about to dive headfirst into the secrets of this place and its arcane Gatekeepers.

Karma didn't waste a second. **"Can you explain how these portals function?"** Her tone was steady, locked onto them with unwavering focus.

Kronos stepped forward, his expression carved from something serious, weighted.

"For the portal to function, it requires three DNA-coded keys—ours. Without them, it remains inert. Each of us carries a corresponding chip beneath our skin. That's the only way to activate the system. No hidden agendas. No corruption."

He and the other Gatekeepers turned their arms, revealing **smooth, circular interfaces embedded into their wrists.** But that wasn't all. Hanging from each of their necks, **a cylindrical key** glinted under the dim light.

I raised an eyebrow. "Still need three controllers, huh? You'd think we'd have a workaround by now. But hey... it is what it is."

And yet, something about it felt **deliberate**. Like the system didn't just require them—it demanded them.

And that raised **more questions than answers.**

"It's been that way because of a turbulent and corrupt past," Sotara, the second Gatekeeper, interjected, her voice carrying the weight of history. "This system ensures that no single individual can wield too much power."

Karma and I exchanged a glance. **Instincts kicking** in.

I folded my arms. "Interesting... I suppose it made sense back then. It was an unstable time."

But history had a way of bleeding **into the present.**

I cut to the chase. "When was the last time the portal was opened?"

Zyna, the third Gatekeeper, didn't hesitate. "We last used it on the 4th of April, a month after the last NexaHunt game."

Karma's posture shifted. Something wasn't adding up. "Then how do you explain recent unauthorized access?"

Her voice sharpened, cutting through the stale air.

Kronos stiffened, disbelief flickering across his face. "Impossible… We would know if someone had tampered with the portal."

"Would they, though?" Karma wasn't letting it slide.

"Are you certain? Could there be a vulnerability in your security measures? **The DNA implants and your keys aren't the only way these portals work, right?** Is there a backup key or an override protocol?"

Sotara's response was instant, unwavering.

"Absolutely not. The portals have been closed. We haven't operated them since April 4th."

I exhaled slowly, shaking my head. "Maybe you didn't know they were being used." I let the thought settle before adding,

"And what about another key? Have you considered the possibility of infiltration? If someone has found a way to bypass your safeguards"

Kronos'and I locked gazes for a brief moment.

"They could be exploiting the portals for something a hell of a lot worse than a game."

The silence that followed wasn't reassuring.

It was ominous.

"Preposterous!" Zyna scoffed, her eyes narrowing.

Classic … Denial … Immediate … Absolute.

But Karma wasn't here to argue.

She was here to uncover the truth.

"Regardless, we must investigate further," she stated, her tone firm. "There's too much at stake to dismiss this matter lightly."

The Gatekeepers exchanged uneasy glances, their confidence fracturing under the weight of our scrutiny. **I could feel the shift, the tension mounting like a coiled wire ready to snap.**

Something was unraveling.

Kronos finally exhaled, his posture stiff with reluctance. "Very well. We will examine our security protocols and review any evidence you may have."

There it was. The first crack in the wall.

I smiled. "Thank you. This investigation has far-reaching implications, and we can't afford to overlook anything."

As if on cue, a guard pulled up a digital tablet, his fingers **dancing** across its surface with mechanical precision. The sterile glow from the screen cast jagged shadows across his face, making the unease in the room **tangible**.

I watched him closely. His brows furrowed in deep concentration, eyes flicking back and forth, scanning.

Karma's patience was **thinning**. "Come on. There must be something in your records."

The guard shook his head, **defeated**. "I started my shift a couple of hours ago, and I haven't seen anything out of the ordinary."

A dead end?

Or just the beginning?

"Shifts are twenty-four hours long, aren't they?" My voice was sharper than I intended, frustration creeping in.

The guard hesitated, shifting uncomfortably. **"Y-yes,"** he stammered, clearly rattled by the intensity in my tone.

"Then give me the log entries."

He paused, fingers tightening around the records like he was second-guessing his next move. But eventually, he handed over a paper copy. I **snatched it up**, scanning the data, my eyes narrowing the further I read.

Something **wasn't right.**

I turned the paper toward Karma, jabbing a finger at the inconsistencies. "Look at this. These don't match the digital records."

She took the document, her gaze steady. "Are you suggesting forgery?"

I exhaled sharply. "Possible. But we need more proof." The pieces were there, scattered, waiting to be put together.

Without hesitation, we both pulled out our high-tech pocket scanners—compact but **powerful** devices, built to detect energy signatures down to the faintest trace. The moment they powered on, a soft hum filled the air, and pale blue light **swept** across the walls, floor, and ceiling.

We worked quickly, methodically.

Then—**a beep.**

"I've got something..." Karma's voice sharpened, her scanner pulsing as it locked onto high-energy signatures—ones that only appeared with recent portal usage.

I stepped closer, watching the readings spike.

"This energy shouldn't still be here unless the portals have been active." Karma's voice carried **undeniable certainty**. She turned to the Gatekeepers, eyes locked on them like a challenge. "Do you know what that means? Over time, these signatures fade. But this? This is fresh."

I folded my arms, letting the weight of her words **sink in.**

Someone had **used** these **portals.**

And the Gatekeepers either didn't know ... or didn't want us to know.

"For example... a frying pan on your stove," Karma continued, keeping her voice even. "Five minutes later, it will still have some heat."

The analogy *hung in the air*, simple yet **undeniable**.

I glanced down at my scanner. Same readings. Same conclusion. "What's going on here?" My voice came out sharper than I intended.

Karma didn't hesitate. "Someone has been using these portals... and they've gone to great lengths to keep it hidden."

The Gatekeepers *looked worried*, you could see it.

Their eyes darting between us and the undeniable evidence pulsing from our devices.

"Impossible!" Kronos' voice wavered, his usual composure cracking. "We've been diligent in our duties. None of us would ever allow such a breach in security!"

But doubt was creeping in, whether he admitted it or not.

Solara seized on that doubt, grasping for an explanation. "It must have been one of the apprentices... they could have opened the portal without permission." His words dripped with **desperation**, like a man trying to outrun the truth.

Kronos *snapped*, eyes flashing. "Are you suggesting my apprentice is responsible? Your own protégé has displayed far more questionable behavior!" His indignation *radiated* through the room, the cracks in their unity widening by the second.

This was unraveling fast.

Karma stepped in before it could spiral further, her calm demeanor standing in **stark contrast** to the growing hysteria. "Enough. Blaming each other won't solve anything."

She let her words settle, then added, "We need to examine all available evidence before jumping to conclusions. It could be something else. Something bigger. And it may not be your apprentices at all."

The room fell **silent**.

A heavy, uneasy silence.

Because deep down, they all knew—this was no accident.

"Agreed. Is there any video surveillance of the portal area that we can review?" I asked, my **patience hanging by a thread.**

Zyna hesitated. Just for a second. But it was enough to confirm what I already suspected—there was more to this than they wanted to admit.

"Yes. We can access the footage in the guard's monitoring room," she finally answered, her voice careful.

She didn't like this.

Neither did I. But for different reasons.

"Lead the way," Karma instructed, her sharp **gaze** *never* leaving the Gatekeepers.

As they guided us through the complex, the tension clung to the air like static before a storm. No one spoke, but every step felt heavier than the last.

(((((O)))))

WHEN WE STEPPED into the **monitoring room**, a dozen screens flickered to life, their eerie glow casting warped shadows along the walls. The hum of active feeds filled the space, an electronic heartbeat pulsing beneath the surface.

Despite the surreal hocus pocus of it all, Karma and I were locked in. **Ready.**

She didn't waste time. "Put on-screen footage corresponding to the unauthorized portal usage."

No argument. No hesitation. The Gatekeepers *complied*. Their fingers danced over the controls, pulling up the data, and then—

The images played.

At first, nothing. Just the empty portal chamber, its cold metallic silence unbroken. Then—*movement*.

"There! Who are they?" I pointed, pulse spiking.

On the screen, a group of men in black suits entered the portal area. Silent. Precise. Like ghosts that weren't supposed to exist. Within seconds, they stepped through one of the inactive portals—and then **disappeared.**

The room stilled.

"I... I don't know them," Kronos stammered. "They're not part of our staff. Nor are they associated with any authorized portal users."

I turned to him, studying the confusion **etched across his face. Genuine.**

Which meant **this went deeper than any of us thought.**

"Unfortunately, the guard on duty during this schedule isn't here." Sotara's voice wavered, uncertainty bleeding through his usually composed tone. "He may know more about these men, but we'll have to wait until he returns to work."

Karma didn't miss a beat. "Very well. In the meantime, gather all the data you can about these individuals and send it to our agency. We'll get to the bottom of this."

I stole one last look at the footage. The grainy image of those suited figures disappearing into the portal *burned into my mind.*

This wasn't just about unauthorized access anymore. This was bigger. **Deeper.** And we were only scratching the surface.

As we stepped out of the monitoring room, the air behind us buzzed with silent tension.

I caught the exchange of uneasy glances between Kronos, Sotara, and Zyna. **They were rattled.** And not just by what they saw, but by what it meant.

Karma folded her arms, waiting.

Finally, Kronos exhaled, rubbing his temple as if the weight of history had suddenly dropped on his shoulders.

"Originally, the portals were designed for exploration — to venture beyond our universe. Later, they became essential for emergency evacuations. And recently... the NexaHunt game. But beyond that? We have no idea how these people gained access."

"Or why they'd even want to use it," Sotara added, voice edged with worry.

Zyna nodded, tension threading through her words.
"Indeed... but rest assured, we will get to the bottom of this and ensure that such breaches never happen again."

I gave a curt nod. "Gotcha."

I glanced at Karma—she gave me the look. We had what we needed. For now.

Without another word, we turned and left.

(((((O)))))

AS WE WALKED AWAY, one thing was clear—we weren't done here.

Not even close.

My thoughts **swirled like a vortex,** spiraling faster the more I tried to make sense of it all. Who the hell were those men in black? What was their purpose? And even more unsettling— who had erased or tampered with the footage?

A deeper, **darker force** was moving beneath the surface, some-thing elusive yet dangerously close to the truth.

I exhaled sharply, my voice cutting through the hum of the complex's generators. "Partner, I have a bad feeling about this. There's something we're missing, something buried just beneath the surface. But what?"

Karma didn't answer right away, but I could feel it—she was thinking the same damn thing.

I let out a slow breath, the weight of everything pressing down on me. Not just the questions, but the gnawing sense that we were missing something—something big. My gaze wasn't on anything in front of me; it was locked on the uncertainty stretching out ahead, just out of reach.

"I don't know," I muttered, dragging a hand over my face. "But... we're about to find out."

We *shared a look*—a silent agreement, unspoken but absolute.

One last glance at the complex, at the Gatekeepers who were shaken but hiding it well, and then we turned and left.

But the question kept hammering in my skull.

Who the hell had used those portals?

And more importantly—who had gone to such extreme lengths to cover it up?

We had enough to take back to HQ, but this wasn't just about data. This was a conspiracy, and I could feel it tightening around us.

We walked towards the **Cloud 9** craft. I stopped and tool a look back at the portal compound. So many thoughts flowed into my mind. I had to snap out of it …

(((((O)))))

WE CLIMBED IN, **powered up the engines, and took off.**

But as the ship cut through the sky, that feeling of accomplishment wasn't as satisfying as it should've been.

Because those men in black had come from somewhere.

And whoever tried to erase them?

They had failed.

Karma flicked my hair as we flew back, smirking. "You need a haircut, Trek. Maybe a little self-care while you're at it."

I cracked a smile before I even realized it. Damn. **She got me.**

She must've noticed too, because her expression shifted just slightly—satisfaction?

Relief? **Go girl,** she was probably thinking.

That's more emotion than I've seen from him in a long time.

We used to do stuff like that—*actual downtime.* Spas. Dinners with Gemma. Sporting events. Concerts. Life outside the mission. That was a different time. A different me.

Karma probably saw an opening now.

A chance to drag me back into something normal.

I wasn't opposed to it—not tonight. The mood was just right. That feeling of accomplishment still clung to us, the kind that only comes after stepping out of **no-man's-land** with more answers than questions.

I sighed, stretching out in my seat. "It was peaceful out there. Calming, in a way."

And just like that, I felt it happening—**I started opening up.**

What I didn't realize—what I never really let myself acknowledge—was how much I'd been affecting everyone around me. I thought I was handling things fine. I stayed on mission. I asked to keep working. I didn't want special treatment. But the truth? I never took the time to grieve.

Losing someone—it changes you. And sometimes, you don't even notice how much.

But if there was one thing I did right, one thing that kept everyone at bay, it was this—I was seeing a therapist **Off-world.**

I figured keeping it off-world meant keeping it private. The last thing I needed was sympathy stares from my own team. If there was one thing I excelled at—one thing I could teach a damn masterclass on—it was how to be discreet.

That wasn't changing anytime soon.

Karma worked her magic, and somehow, I ended up agreeing to a damn haircut.

No resistance, no argument. I knew I needed one, and honestly? It wasn't worth the fight. She called up her friend Marcie, set it all up, and just like that—I was locked in.

But I should've known better.

Because Karma wasn't just planning a haircut. She was up to something.

She was being sneaky, **too sneaky**, and I could feel it. That subtle excitement in her voice, the way she wasn't looking me directly in the eye. She had *an agenda*.

And I was about to walk straight into it.

She was prepping me for something—**a night out.** Only, I didn't know it yet.

Karma wanted fun, energy, music—one last wild night before we left for NexaHunt Studios the next day. And apparently, I was going to be part of that plan, whether I knew it or not.

She had a whole setup brewing in her head.

Her martial arts actress friend, Yeowang, was in town. So was another close friend. They were already set on hitting the clubs.

And Karma? She was determined to make sure I came along.

Not just for the drinks and the music. Not just because she wanted me to *loosen the hell up for once.*

She needed me on this mission.

And I was still on the fence.

But that? That was about to change.

PART TWO
THE JOURNEY BEGINS

CHAPTER 5
TECH & CEYLON

WE STEPPED INTO THE LAB.

Ambient hum, neon glows, the faint scent of metal, fluid, and wiring.

It was subtle, but once you noticed it, **you never forgot**.

The place was packed with high-tech machinery and experimental prototypes—some Federation-approved, others probably *not. Holographic data streams pulsed across transparent screens*, forming a digital haze that flickered across the walls.

Dexx was exactly where we expected—hunched over his workstation, tinkering with some device that looked important. His **sharp eyes reflected the glow of the holograms**, locked in, laser-focused.

The lab's AI announced our arrival, and he pulled off his headphones without looking up.

Dexx. The guy looked like a **Viking who took a detour through a cyberwarfare program**—tall, ex-military build, all that. But instead of wielding an axe, he built *game-changing tech*. That was his war now.

And underneath all the engineering genius, I knew why he did it. **Agent 424.**

MIA. Years ago. Lost on a mission that should've been routine. Dexx never stopped searching. And if he couldn't find him? He'd make damn sure no one else from ISAD suffered the same fate.

Dexx's voice cut through the hum of the lab.

"Agent Trek. Karma. Right on time."

He gestured toward his sleek, **frosted-glass workstation—** gadgets and devices spread across it in a deliberate pattern, like weapons laid out before battle.

"I've got some new toys for you."

The first thing he picked up was a set of **HoloEye Implants—** small, sleek, no bigger than contact lenses. Under the bright lab lights, they shimmered like liquid crystal

He handed me one of the **Implants**, *no larger than a contact lens.*

"These will record data in real-time," Dexx explained, watching me turn it over between my fingers. "Everything you see, mission central sees."

I lifted it closer to my eye. **Damn. Small, but intricate.** The level of tech packed into this thing was unreal.

Dexx continued, "They also offer **night vision, thermal imaging, and a built-in heads-up display for tactical data.** Think of it as an upgrade to the *ThermoHoloSpecs* you used on your last mission."

I caught the way he *watched my reaction.* The Specs weren't just a tool—they were a crutch. A controlled feed of reality, but also a record of everything I missed the first time.

"What's the range?" I asked, voice even.

"Unlimited," Dexx said. "As long as you're near a portal or linked satellite."

Next, he picked up a **small metallic chip**, its **surface pulsing faintly** with embedded tech.

"NeuroSync Implants," he said. "They store everything your brain processes. Memory logs. Data retrieval. If you see it, hear it, or think about it, headquarters can pull it up later."

Karma gave a slow nod, **impressed.** "That's a game changer."

Dexx's smirk told me he wasn't done. He reached for the ultimate device—a *thin, disc-like implant* glowing with a subtle, *otherworldly energy.*

"This one," he said, **holding it up between two fingers**, "will keep your mind sane while you're on Earth."

Karma tensed slightly. I did too.

Dexx tapped the implant against his palm. "Beta Mind Deflector. Blocks mind control, psychic attacks, and telepathic intrusions." His gaze flicked up to me. "You're gonna need it."

He gestured for us to sit.

I barely had time to settle before he pressed something cold against the **base of my skull**—just above the hairline.

A sharp click.

A brief pressure.

Then a *tingling sensation* spread across my scalp, threading into my neural pathways like invisible filaments.

The Beta Mind Deflector Implant was active.

I exhaled, rolling my shoulders as my mind adjusted to the foreign presence inside it. There was no pain, just a subtle awareness—like a faint, unreadable signal humming at the edge of my perception.

Karma touched the back of her neck. "That's … weird."

"Yeah," I muttered, flexing my fingers. The tingling was already fading, but the implant was **there**—woven into my nervous system now. Permanent.

Dexx smirked. "You'll thank me later."

I met his gaze. "Sounds like we're going in fully loaded."

"Almost." He reached for something else on the table, *his fingers brushing over two sleek black alloy bands*. The slightest grin tugged at the corner of his mouth as he held one up between his fingers.

"These may look like simple wrist jewelry," he said, pausing just long enough for the tease to land. "But they're *so* much more than that."

He slid one across the table toward me. "Go on. Try it."

I picked it up. Cool metal. Lighter than it looked.

Karma was already fastening hers. The moment the band locked around my wrist, **a soft blue glow pulsed to life,** tracing a slow-moving infinity symbol across the surface—like it was *breathing*.

I turned my wrist, watching how the glow responded— pulsing slightly in sync with my movements, like it could **read me**.

The lab table flickered, its smooth surface shifting as it trans- formed into a holographic interface. Blueprints and schematics emerged from thin air, rotating **suspended in mid-space**.

On the far side of the projection, Dexx's image materialized, semi-transparent in blue light.

His voice came through crisp. "Pay attention."

The tone was smooth. Authoritative.

"These devices are multi-functional," Dexx continued, his holographic form pacing across the display. "But they *shine* when activated."

He tapped his wrist.

With a soft click, the device **came alive.**

Two sleek segments unfurled—one sliding across his palm like a black gauntlet, the other rising just above his wrist.The components moved with an elegant, machine-like precision, alloy plates adjusting and locking into place with a faint, synchronized glow.

"All connected," Dexx said, flexing his fingers. "The material's a composite alloy—lightweight, adaptable, but strong as hell. It moves with you, reacts to you. The **inner layer?** Flexible, almost rubber-like. That's what gives it full range of motion."

Then his smirk sharpened.

"Now, watch closely."

At the far end of the lab, a **target flickered into existence**—a glowing holographic silhouette, shifting between solid and translucent.

Dexx raised his arm, movements sharp, controlled. A *low hum* built up inside the device, like a power source priming itself.

Then—**a pulse of pure energy** launched from his wrist.

A streak of blue light cut across the lab, hitting the target dead center. The impact exploded outward in a shockwave of glowing digital fragments, scattering like shattered glass before vanishing into the air.

The silence that followed was thick, humming with static from the shot's residual charge.

I let out a low whistle, eyes still locked on the **smoking remnants**.

"Yeah … *not just jewelry.*"

Karma tilted her head, arms crossed. "I'll admit, that's impressive." A beat. "But how long before *we* get a chance to try?"

Dexx smirked as he powered down the device. The sleek components **retracted seamlessly** back into the wristband, vanishing like they had never been there.

"Soon enough," he said. "Master it first, and you'll realize it's not just a weapon—it's an **extension of you.**"

His smirk faded, replaced by something **more serious.**

"But not in the *NexaHunt game.* These devices are **prohibited** there for obvious reasons. You'll pick yours up from your MIB handlers once you're back on Earth. They'll keep them **secured** until you're ready."

I exchanged a glance with Karma. Good to know.

Dexx folded his arms, nodding. "Now, you're ready to begin your mission." His voice held a **hint of pride**, but mostly **a warning.**

"Just make sure you bring everything back in one piece. These aren't exactly replaceable."

Before we could turn to leave, he reached for something else—a **pair of small, metallic discs** no bigger than coins.

"Here," he said, handing us each two. "**TraceBeacons.** Could come in handy."

Karma rolled one between her fingers. "*TraceBeacons?*"

Dexx nodded. "They **sync to all your gear**—trackable, retrievable, and they can be **remotely activated** if you ever need a location beacon. Use them wisely."

I clenched mine in my palm. **A small tool, but possibly a lifesaver.**

"Appreciate it, Dexx," I said, sliding them into my pocket. "We'll bring everything back in one piece."

Dexx's smirk returned. "See that you do."

With that, we were locked and loaded. Time to move.

Just before we stepped out of the lab, something caught my eye.

In the far corner, parked under a web of glowing data panels and **dangling cables,** was something that didn't belong.

Sleek. Chrome. Alive!

It looked like a silver Porsche 356 Speedster convertible—except it had been ripped straight from the fever dream of a mad scientist on intra-dimensional steroids.

The **liquid-metal surface** gleamed like **mercury in motion,** subtly shifting shades as the overhead lights **pulsed.**

And it wasn't sitting on the floor.

It **hovered.**

The tires had folded seamlessly into the body at a 45-degree angle, leaving it suspended just inches above the polished obsidian floor. A faint hum resonated from it—not a sound, exactly, but a vibration at the edge of perception, like a barely there frequency waiting to be heard.

I slowed my pace, letting Karma stride a few steps ahead before stopping completely.

Didn't even try to hide my awe.

I moved closer, tilting my head, inspecting it like a piece of fine art.

"Beautiful, isn't she?"

Dexx's voice cut through the **sterile hum** of the lab.

I barely noticed him appear beside me, hands tucked casually into his coat pockets, watching my reaction like he already knew the effect this thing had on people. A **smirk** tugged at the corner of his mouth.

"We call it the **Parallax Speeder.**"

Behind me, Karma stopped, realizing I wasn't following.

She doubled back, arms crossed. "We're *on the clock*, Trek."

"Hold up." I didn't take my eyes off the Speeder.

"This thing looks like it belongs in a **museum**—or on the **cover of a rock album.**"

I glanced sideways at Dexx. **"What's it doing here?"**

Dexx chuckled softly, stepping closer to the Speeder.

"This isn't just a pretty face," he said, placing a hand on the hood.

The **metal rippled beneath his touch—like liquid responding to heat.**

"The **Parallax** is the pinnacle of interdimensional engineering. Open a portal," he said, **fingers trailing across the surface**, "and this beauty will take you through *seamlessly.*"

I let out a low whistle, fingers **gliding along the side of the car.** The surface was **cool, unnervingly smooth**—like it wasn't metal at all.

More like something **alive.**

"Portal travel, huh?" I muttered. "Sounds like it could come in handy. **What else can it do?**"

Dexx's smirk widened, like he'd been waiting for that question.

"It's equipped with a **built-in force field**—activates automatically if it detects an attack."

I glanced up. "**Automatic?**"

He nodded. "Plasma rounds? Particle beams? Even **dimensional distortions**—it'll **absorb or deflect** them without a scratch." He let that sink in before adding, **"And before you ask, yes—it's faster than anything you've ever driven."**

I smirked. "I'd love to test that."

Behind me, Karma folded her arms. "I'm guessing there's a catch. There always is."

Dexx turned to her, nodding like he expected the skepticism.

"Sharp as ever, Agent Karma. The **Parallax is still a prototype.** No field tests. No combat data. Consider this…" His smirk returned. "A **preview** of what's coming."

I stepped back, eyes still locked on the Speeder.

This was more than just a vehicle.

This was the bleeding edge of interdimensional travel. And if it worked the way Dexx claimed, it wasn't just an asset—it was a game changer.

Karma groaned. "Great. *Look at him.*"

She shot Dexx a knowing look, then turned back to me—**eyes narrowed, arms crossed.**

"You're already picturing yourself behind the wheel, aren't you?"

I didn't even try to deny it.

Instead, I grinned and slid into the driver's seat as the Parallax lowered slightly, adjusting for my entry.

The interior pulsed to life.

Holographic controls materialized around me—floating dials, light-etched displays shifting to my presence. The cockpit felt like something **straight out of a dream**, smooth panels curving seamlessly around me.

"Holy shit," I muttered, fingers hovering over the **illuminated console.**

Karma rolled her eyes but smirked despite herself.

"Alright, buddy," she said, grabbing the top of the door and leaning in slightly. "La La Land's over. We gotta go."

(((((O)))))

THE **DRENCHED** streets of the **party district** pulsed with life.

Limos lined both sides of the road, their polished surfaces **catching the electric glow of the city**. Camera flashes went off in rapid succession—**paparazzi swarming like vultures**, their lenses snapping up every scandal, every drunken slip, every high-profile moment.

Which led us to *Yeowang*.

A hot, sexy, out-of-control storm of a woman.

You couldn't miss her. No one could.

She was waiting outside, **basking in the chaos**—posing with a **devious smile,** working the cameras like they owed her something.

That bright yellow patent leather dress?

It clung to her like **a second skin**—so short that it barely covered anything. It wasn't a dress—it was a publicity weapon.

Karma and I exchanged a glance.

Yeah, she knew exactly what she was doing.

Her new movie was coming out. This was *free marketing*, and every single flash of a camera was another ticket sold.

$(((((O)))))$

THE SECOND we stepped into Club Ceylon, the air snapped with electricity. Place had only been open a week, and it was already breaking records. This wasn't just a club—it was a body-packed *temple of excess*.

And tonight?

The NexaHunt party was about to make history.

The pulse of the club hit like a body blow—heat and movement wrapped around us. Half-naked bodies grinding under holographic spotlights, the rhythm crawling through the floor and up my spine.

Models. Movie stars. Musicians. Photographers. Artists.

Every direction I looked — someone famous, someone reckless.

Android bartenders ghosted through the chaos, synthetic limbs fluid, pouring drinks like machines possessed.

The bar? Already a war-zone.

Getting a drink was a damn sport.

We shoved through the press of bodies; the bass pounding through my ribs, yelling orders over the beat.

The whole place was alive—glowing, humid, bodies undulating like liquid heat.

Karma and I soaked it in. The green-lit aquariums lined the club, dancers inside moving like otherworldly creatures behind glass. The glow painted their silhouettes in hypnotic ripples—every curve, every motion amplified by water and light.

And Yeowang? Totally unique.

Her eyes darted between the two DJs, battling it out.

To the right—DJ NRG, relentless. His beats cracked like thunder.

To the left—DJ Kidd, all swagger, slicing the air with a razor-sharp mix.

They were both murdering it.

The music wasn't just noise—it was sensation. Sweat, skin, rhythm, sex. Fused together and feeding off each other.

Primal. Hypnotic. Alive.

Heat and sound seeped into me, thick and slow like honey laced with static. The crowd pulsed, nearly vibrating.

Some women wore tassels. Some wore less than that.

Some were just straight-up naked.

"So hot," Karma murmured, her voice low, eyes sweeping the scene.

I nodded. **Hell yes.**

And the men? Whoa.

Muscles on muscles on muscles.

Yeowang finally scored her drink—a radioactive-looking green potion. Karma's was deep, electric blue. They glowed like alien cocktails.

She looked at me, eyebrow cocked. "You sure you don't want one?"

I shook my head. **Nah.** Last night gave me all the alcohol I needed.

No, bitch. Not again.

We leaned into the bar, the crowd undulating around us—skin on skin, flirtation in the air, conversations dripping with heat and promise.

A man and woman moved toward us. Confident. Purposeful.

He smiled—*that* kind of smile. Not just a "can I buy you a drink?" smile.

It was an **invitation**.

Karma and Yeowang locked eyes—one of those silent bestie exchanges.

Answer: Declined.

Instead, we let ourselves get pulled deeper into the current— the pulse of the club, the seductive hum of being wanted but choosing *not* to be claimed.

"Girl…" Yeowang giggled, nudging Karma. "Can you believe they want this hottie?"

Karma laughed, shaking her head. "Girl, you need to stop." Her eyes flicked around, wide, a little on edge.

Yeowang sipped her drink, completely unbothered. "Nah, don't stop," she teased.

Karma gave her a look. "I wasn't about to."

Yeowang puckered her lips. "Good."

A shiver crawled up my spine.

Goosebumps exploded across my skin—instant, electric. Like the universe whispering in code only my nerves could hear.

Something wasn't right.

Or maybe ... something was about to be *very* right.

The air in Club Ceylon thickened—vibrating, almost. My gaze swept the crowd. Flashing lights. Pounding rhythm.

Then—*the pull.*

Not physical. Not rational. Just real.

A force locked onto me. Not my body—*my life-force.*

Yeowang, still vibing to the beat, noticed my freeze-frame.

"Boi," she said, snapping her gum, "you glitching out?" she added as the beat of the music pulsed with the rhythm of my heartbeat.

Karma turned, concern flashing in her eyes.

But I couldn't answer. I wasn't even here anymore.

Because then—*she* appeared.

She walked through the club like the laws of physics made an exception for her.

Hair like silver light, streaked with solar flare orange.

Rose-tinted glasses.

Golden amulet.

Lion emblem.

Eyes full of stars.

She didn't just glow—she **remembered**.

She remembered *me*.

For a heartbeat, I felt exposed—like someone had pulled a cosmic file on me and started reading aloud.

Yeowang was already **smitten with her aura.**

And I wasn't far behind.

She turned to Yeowang, voice smooth as velvet folded in moonlight.

"Would you like a palm reading? Or the tarot?"

"I'm Lunara," she said. Vibe resonated with ours. "I'm the best in the universe."

Yeowang, never one to hesitate, **slapped her palm forward.** "Hit me."

Lunara glanced at it only briefly before smiling.

"You're about to come into a lot of money."

Yeowang squealed. "That movie better, *pop*, huh?" She winked and vanished back into the crowd.

But Lunara didn't move.

She turned back to me. And leaned in.

Not close enough to touch, but enough for the noise around us to *dim*. Like reality held its breath.

"You're not ready yet," she said, eyes peering through me like I was made of glass.

"For what?" I asked, voice unsteady.

Her smile deepened, sad and knowing.

"You'll understand ... in the *other* world."

My thoughts fractured.

Other world? Did she mean a dream? A parallel realm? A metaphor?

But before I could ask, she was gone.

Not walked away—just… **absent**. Like a channel turned off mid-broadcast.

I looked down at my empty hand.

Expecting something.

No idea what.

But whatever it was … it wasn't time.

(((((O)))))

WHEN WE FINALLY STEPPED OUTSIDE the club, the early morning air hit like a splash of cold water—sharp, sobering, refreshing.

"Faaahhh! *What time is it?*" Yeowang groaned, her voice slurred but still dramatic.

I was **lost in my thoughts**, my mind looping through *foretold futures and paths I hadn't yet walked.*

But not *too* lost.

I smirked. "It's 3:33 a.m., you little whore."

Yeowang cackled, hanging off Karma like a human scarf, her balance clearly *on its last life.*

The music from Club Ceylon still thumped through the streets, distant but alive, the neon glow painting the sidewalks in liquid color.

We stood there, waiting for the limo, the city humming around us.

And deep in my core, I felt it.

That **shift.** That undeniable sense that everything was about to change.

Like this night wasn't just a night—**it was the prelude to something bigger.**

Something that would alter the **very fabric of my reality.**

The city lights blurred past as we rode through the streets, but my mind wasn't in the car.

It was still back there—with Lunara.

With her **words, her presence, her warning.**

"The journey is yours. Step into it. Control it. And see the world with brand-new eyes."

I closed my eyes.

I had no idea what was coming.

But I knew one thing.

I was about to find out.

(((((O)))))

I HAD **a lot to think about** the moment I got home. Lunara's words still echoed in my head. So did Director Nyx's offer.

ISAD. The mission. **The choice.**

It looped through my mind, over and over, until it became **noise.**

I needed peace … I made myself a margarita and checked out for a minute. I never drank alone. Never felt the need.

But this? **This was different.**

The stakes were too high. **Save a friend and get suckered into ISAD.**

I needed clarity. **Answers.**

But the drink wasn't going to give me that.

It was only going to put me to sleep.

Maybe that's what I needed—to just **sleep it off.**

Except … **I couldn't.**

The thoughts wouldn't stop.

I paced through my home, **moving from room to room**, trying to shake the feeling that I'd made a mistake.

Agreeing to join ISAD.

I told myself I was ready. **But was I?**

This wasn't the first time I thought about walking away from the Special Forces Division. That thought had crept up for years, mission after mission.

It wasn't new.

But this time … **this time, it felt final.**

A slow weight settled in my chest—the kind I had felt before.

The kind that made me retreat, isolate. The kind that turned my world inward.

Depression. **Reclusion.**

My steps slowed.

And then I noticed **Bebe watching me.**

She had been silent this whole time, her presence subtle but observant.

Waiting.

AI never spoke unless necessary. She was **calculating the perfect moment.**

And then—

"I… I've got five hours to decide, or they're gonna send someone else."

My voice came out uneven, like the thought **was heavier out loud than in my head.**

A brief silence.

Then, finally, **Bebe spoke.**

"What seems to be your dilemma?"

"Gemma is missing."

"I understand. Did you not end your military career?"

"I did, but…" I exhaled, running a hand over my face. "I feel like I made the wrong decision."

"With ending your commission?"

"No." I shook my head. "They recruited me into ISAD… and now I wish I hadn't joined. I'm torn. Director Nyx gave me 24 hours to decide."

Bebe's voice remained **calm, calculated.**

"She is giving you a choice for a reason. She senses your hesitation."

I frowned. "Why though? They've never given me a choice before."

A pause.

Then Bebe asked, "Are you in top mental and physical shape for this?"

The question hit harder than I expected.

I glanced around the room, *my thoughts circling like vultures.*

Was I?

A beat of silence stretched between us. Bebe **waited.**

Finally, I inhaled, straightened my shoulders. "I am. I'm fit."

The words felt automatic, like muscle memory. But saying it didn't make it feel true.

I called Karma … … …

CHAPTER 6
IT BEGINS

TODAY WAS THE DAY.

By the end of it, we'd be through the portal—the mission in full motion.

I stared out the window of the **hoverbus**, watching the passing landscape blur by. My mind was steady. My decision made.

And all the noise inside the bus?

It would all be **justified** the moment I brought Gemma back home.

The energy in the hoverbus was in **a frenzy.** Contestants—hyped, eager, loud. They were here to win, to compete.

The buzz of their voices took me back—to grade school trips, packed buses, kids bouncing in their seats, ready for an adventure.

Except this? This wasn't a game.

The itinerary was strict, intentional. Every pickup point, every scheduled stop—the organizers weren't just coordinating a competition.

They were controlling the movement of every single person involved.

And that? That was the simple part.

The hoverbus **hissed** to a stop. The sleek doors slid open.

Karma stepped inside, eyes sharp, energy dialed up and ready.

The last one to board.

Our journey was now **in motion.**

I sat near the front, staring ahead, keeping my expression neutral.

Karma took a seat one row behind me. Close enough that I could sense her presence, but far enough that we might as well have been strangers.

The illusion held.

The mission had **officially begun.**

The low drone of engines filled the air as the hoverbus began its journey to NexaHunt Studios—the place where the ultimate adventure awaited.

When we arrived, two other hoverbuses were already lined up ahead of us, idling in place like coiled beasts waiting for release.

All three buses represented contestants from three different planets. All of us—lined up, sealed in, waiting.

The drivers checked their **wristwatches.** Their eyes locked onto the second hand, counting down to exactly 9:00 a.m.

Not a second sooner.

The air inside the bus felt **thick, charged.**

Outside, three **game greeters** stood in position at the three entrance doors. Their outfits were ornate, surreal—gowns shaped like inverted cones, wide at the bottom, tapering toward their necks. Their headpieces? Intricate metal spheres, almost hypnotic in their design.

They stood completely still. **Waiting.**

We all were.

Then—the moment hit.

The second hand reached twelve.

9:00 a.m. sharp.

The hoverbus doors slid open in unison.

Chaos exploded.

Contestants surged forward, shoving, sprinting toward the building.

The first fifty inside would win immunity—a golden advantage in the game. Every second mattered.

I moved with the crowd, dodging elbows, keeping Karma in my periphery.

Then—the ground shifted.

No.

The ground opened.

A deep, gut-wrenching *CRACK* echoed through the air as the pavement beneath us **split apart—sharp, jagged, alive.**

Like the **snapping jaws of a predator.** A crocodile pit, swallowing people whole.

Screams cut through the chaos. Contestants tripped, tumbled—

some barely catching the edges, others disappearing into the gaping abyss below.

And then—

A **giggle.**

Sharp. High-pitched. **Deliberate.**

One of the **game greeters—stone-faced, elegant, monstrous in her surreal gown—tilted her head slightly.**

And **giggled**.

Just once.

Like the screams were… **entertaining.**

A cold weight settled in my stomach.

This wasn't just a competition.

This was NexaHunt. Bitch!

Contestants **scrambled** to get out of the pit, arms clawing at the netting around the perimeter. **Frantic. Desperate.**

I laughed, swinging myself up with ease, Karma right behind me.

We were **out first.**

The greeters—**still eerily composed** despite the chaos—handed us ribbons, marking us for entry into the studio.

(((((O)))))

INSIDE, the shift was instant.

A **pulse of bass-heavy, trance-like music** vibrated through the space, wrapping around the crowd like a spell.

At the center of it all—**Lyra Starweaver and Zane Astren.** The host and co-host.

They danced atop their glowing platforms, their movements **fluid, magnetic**, while behind them, a team of **professional dancers** moved in sync—every step precise, choreographed to perfection.

Their presence was pure electricity.

Not just for us—but for the entire audience watching from home.

Everything about the show was designed to **pull you in.**

The entire experience unfolded like a live documentary, every angle covered by **spherical drones** floating seamlessly through the air—capturing every moment of excitement, every expression, every heartbeat of anticipation.

And all of this?

All of this was happening before we had even entered the studio.

Then came — **the ritual.**

One by one, contestants were instructed to **strip down** and step into a **pristine, white, glowing cube.**

No instructions. No explanations.

Just **disrobe and enter.**

The cube was **silent, waiting.**

Inside, a warm, **faintly pulsing light** enveloped each contestant as the *advanced scanning system mapped every inch of their bodies.*

No margin for error. No room for deception.

Outside, **medical assistants stood by**, monitoring **data feeds in real time.**

Anyone flagged with **health concerns?**

Separated. Removed from the process.

Swift. Efficient. **Cold.**

The rest?

Deemed fit to continue.

(((((O)))))

AFTER RETRIEVING OUR CLOTHES, we lined up to **sign the waivers.**

The music still pulsed through the lobby, rhythmic, intoxicating. The dancers? Still moving like they could do this forever.

Excitement buzzed in the air—**thick, undeniable.**

I kept a safe distance from Karma, watching her from the corner of my eye.

Either she was **acting** or she was **actually overwhelmed.**

Hard to tell.

And honestly? **I didn't blame her.**

The sheer number of contestants—packed into this ultramodern beast of a studio, inside the most futuristic city in the galaxy—was overwhelming as hell.

Karma looked **in awe.**

Me? **Not impressed.**

I glanced up. The studio's ceiling stretched impossibly high, a towering cathedral of tech and spectacle.

Suspended overhead, interdimensional pods hung from thick, gleaming silver cables, each pod marked with a number.

Each one was a **vessel.**

A transport.

A portal.

These pods had *carried past contestants to parallel worlds*—flung them into the echoes of the past, the **fractures of time.**

And here I was.

Pretending to be one of them.

I exhaled. You gotta do what you gotta do.

As we moved through the crowd of contestants, the scale of the studio pressed in from all sides.

Massive monitors lined the walls, towering and alive—displaying holographic footage of past NexaHunt players, their forms flickering mid-action as they navigated impossible landscapes, dodged death, outplayed fate.

Everywhere I looked, contestants from **Chronoria, Nexotara, and Zenexis** whispered in hushed tones, their faces tense with nerves, their mouths parted in stunned silence.

Some looked terrified.

Some looked hungry for the challenge.

I watched them, studying their reactions, letting their unease settle over me like a cold current beneath all the artificial energy.

Because whatever happened next?

The real game hadn't even begun yet.

The signing station loomed ahead—a sleek, curved structure embedded with state-of-the-art biometric pens pulsing with soft blue light.

I barely noticed the line.

My attention locked onto the open pod displayed on the studio floor—its silver exterior gleaming under the overhead lights.

Sleek. Waiting. A **doorway into the unknown.**

For me, this wasn't a game.

This was a **mission. Find Gemma. Find the missing players. Get them home.**

I stepped forward, gripping the biometric pen.

The neon pulse flickered beneath my fingers.

I had no choice. It was part of the plan.

"Next," a robotic-sounding voice called out.

I signed. Sealed my fate.

I glanced toward Karma in the distance.

She looked **eager, amped.** Her energy was different—**buzzing, ready.**

For her, this wasn't some high-stakes operation.

This was **a thrill. A story to tell later.**

She grabbed the biometric pen and scrawled her signature across the waiver. The glow of the tablet flashed across her face as she smirked, stepping forward to join the others.

The other contestants were just as wired, feeding off the high-voltage anticipation.

The lobby pulsed with movement. The holographic monitors

towered over us, flickering with footage of past NexaHunt players—dodging, fighting, surviving.

I took it all in, knowing that beyond these walls...

The real game was waiting.

I had been **taking mental notes** since stepping onto the hoverbus.

Every detail. Every interaction.

Each one synced into the AI implant in my head, stored in a digital notepad connected to the source.

It was new tech, something Karma and I were testing. We were the first subjects for it—a direct feed that synchronized data before uploading it to a collector at mission control.

Nyx had access before anyone.

Top-secret clearance had its perks.

(((((O)))))

THE SESSION KEPT ROLLING, but the energy in the room had shifted.

That wide-eyed awe?

Gone. Now it buzzed—**focused, electric, ready for war.**

Everyone felt it. The stakes were real, and the tools we'd just been handed? No longer toys. They were survival.

Orientation hit, and I'd been logging mental notes since stepping onto that damn hoverbus. Fed them straight into the AI implant behind my ear like a junkie feeding data into the void.

Karma and I were beta testing this neural gear—first gen, straight from the lab. We were the canaries in the mine. Every sync went to a collector node at mission control, Nyx getting first dibs on the feed. Top-secret clearance came with its perks, apparently.

(((((O)))))

THE SECOND we entered the training room, the lights flared to life—**giant displays snapping on with simulations of the parallel worlds ahead**. Hazy, surreal, glitching slightly at the edges like they knew what kind of chaos waited inside them.

Lyra and Zane stood posted up on a platform flanked by instructors. They didn't say much, just waited with that look—**calm, cold, calculated.** Every piece of gear laid out was mission critical. We knew that. Hell, we felt it.

I caught movement across the room. Kaya.

Gliding through the crowd like she owned the damn frequency. Couldn't help the way my pulse ticked up a notch. Her energy? Aligned. Potential ally, maybe more.

Strategy or distraction—still undecided.

Then—**bam**—some other contestant smacked straight into me, lost in her own orbit.

My reflexes kicked in. Hand out, steadying her. "Whoa, gurl ... Watch where you're going." I flashed her a grin.

She blushed hard, brushing hair behind one ear. "Sorry about that," she mumbled, cheeks flushed. Could feel the heat rising from her skin where I'd touched her.

Karma, walking beside me, snorted. "Smooth move, Trek. You know she plays for my team, don't you?"

"No way," I shot back with a smirk.

"I'm just keeping our cover intact ... **strategizing.**"

I winked at Kaya before shifting focus. Had to stay sharp.

(((((O)))))

THE ROOM PACKED IN.

Zane took the floor—commanding, cool, like a man who's seen some shit. The wrist-comm devices were next. Multi-tools for nav, updates, tracking, and artifact pings. High-tech as hell.

The others? Practically drooling over the thing.

Zane broke it down—real-time translation, mind-linked UI, **mental command recognition**.

Asta backed him up, fingers dancing over the surface, spinning up a hologram like it was nothing. The glow lit her hands, casting fractured shadows like something out of a dream.

"This is the HoloComm Wrist Device," she said. "More than comms—it's your everything."

Zane added the key moves: double-tap for messages, triple for stealth mode. "It reads your thoughts," he said, tone low. "But it also tracks you. Lose it? You're compromised. **Guard it like your life depends on it—because it does.**"

Yeah, message received.

(((((O)))))

NEXT CAME THE MOBILE PORTAL.

Asta lifted what looked like a designer belt, but that sucker had glowing seams, faint but pulsing. Zane called it what it was—an escape route. Activate, visualize, jump.

She hit the button, and **the air tore open in front of her—** colors bleeding into a swirling vortex. The hum it gave off crawled across my skin.

"You get five uses," Zane warned. "After that, it's fashion only. And no backtracking. One way through. That's it."

Damn. No room for hesitation.

(((((O)))))

ZANE'S VOICE BOOMED: "Get familiar with your gear!"

We swarmed the tables. Sleek tech lined up, waiting to bond with us. Asta handed me the wrist device, and I latched it on. Cool metal against my skin. Kaya activated hers first—soft hum, then light. "Whoa, this is amazing," she whispered.

Asta guided her through the interface. The system felt *alive*.

I frowned as I tapped mine. "What happens if this thing glitches mid-game?"

Zane chuckled. "We tested it in harsher conditions than you'll face. If it fails, the portal compensates."

Right. Totally comforting.

Asta passed around the belts. Zelara clicked hers on. "Let's see what this baby can do." Portal opened—boom—she was across the room, grinning wide.

I tested mine. Didn't step through, just needed to feel it hum. Strategic. Tactical.

Zane reminded us—limited range. **Don't blow it on drama.**

(((((O)))))

THEN CAME THE DRONES.

Tiny things—sleek, light, alive. Asta cracked open a crate and let them loose.

"Scout ahead," Kaya said. Hers zipped forward, beaming live feed back to her wrist. Blue glow pulsing like a heartbeat.

I pushed mine harder. "Drone, return." It arced back clean. Efficient.

Then—**spark, pop, smoke.** One of the wrist devices failed. Contestant flinched.

Asta didn't flinch. "Minor malfunction. Early-phase stuff."

But the tension was there. We all felt it. Even the top tech had cracks.

(((((O)))))

THEN IT WAS TIME.

The center of the room. Tubes—**tall, translucent, glowing softly like they breathed.** I stepped closer. The hum beneath my feet vibrated through my bones.

Zane and Asta flanked the pods.

"These sequence your body," Zane said. "Protect your mind. Arm your spirit."

Asta nodded. "Symbiosis. You'll feel it."

One by one, people stepped in. Light swallowed them. Heartbeat synced with tech. Images, symbols, code **slammed into them**—too fast to catch.

Then—**doorways of light. Subtle. Flickering. Whispering.**

"Remember everything. Count the doorways. They will lead you back."

My turn.

Inside the tube, heat surged. Light bled into my skin. The message hit. One. Two. Three doorways. *Imprinted.*

I stepped out. **Different. Tuned. Upgraded. A little haunted.**

Zane closed it down. "You're ready. Just don't forget—this isn't just physical. It's mental. Psychological. Existential."

No kidding.

(((((O)))))

ZANE LED us through a narrow corridor—walls glowing like veins.

The floor pulsed under my boots. We stepped into the Briefing Room. Glass walls. Massive screens. Air so still it felt held by a breath.

Lyra stood, waiting.

Tall. Commanding. Eyes that saw through timelines.

She didn't welcome us like a host—she *declared* the start of something dangerous.

Earth rotated behind her on the screen. She broke it down:

Geopolitical collapse. Religious chaos. Climate catastrophe.

Shadow regimes. Sky Being cults. Factions worshipping ancient tech like gods.

"Water is worth more than gold," she said.

"Time travelers. Ultraterrestrials. Hidden agendas."

I saw it in everyone's eyes—Kaya's especially. Doubt. Resolve. Fear.

Lyra's tone shifted. She walked to a table of gear.

"These are your survival kits. Learn them. Trust no one. Not even yourselves."

This was no game. Not anymore.

And me?

I was ready.

CHAPTER 7
THE LOUNGE

THE PURPLE LIGHT draped the lounge in an **otherworldly glow**, flickering against holographic replays of past NexaHunt finales.

The hum of unseen tech filled the space, mixing with hushed conversations, scattered laughter, and the subtle tension of contestants masking their nerves.

I barely blinked, but my **eye implants auto-calibrated**, feeding me real-time enhancements of the room. Facial recognition. Micro-expressions. Audio filters isolating key voices. Dexx's tech was running smooth, no lag.

The **floor-to-ceiling windows** framed a sprawling cityscape, the deep-red velvet curtains embroidered with geometric gold patterns giving the place an odd blend of luxury and high-tech paranoia.

Kaya Kellix.

My gaze locked onto her for a fraction of a second—just enough to activate my implant's auditory relay. A soft click in my earpiece. Connection secured.

She reached for a cup of coffee—bumped into **Nenah Nova.**

The cup wobbled. Near spill.

"Sorry about that," Kaya said, flashing a quick smile.

Nenah returned it, easy. "No worries."

A chuckle passed between them. A moment of relief before the game turned them into enemies.

Karma, seated near me, barely moved. Her posture was relaxed, but I felt her scan the room too—her implants tracking, listening.

"First time here?" Kaya stirred her coffee, eyes flicking to Nenah.

"Yeah, you?" Nenah's voice had a **micro-hitch of uncertainty.**

"Same. It's a lot to take in." Kaya's fingers tapped her cup. A nervous tick. Doubt creeping in.

I tuned into the frequency. **Heart rate slightly elevated.** But not high enough to be outright fear—**more like calculated wariness.**

"Mind if we find a quieter spot to talk?" Kaya asked.

Nenah hesitated. **A beat too long.**

She's debating something. **Why engage with Kaya? Trust her, or keep her close?**

Then she nodded. Decision made.

They moved toward one of the deep-purple couches tucked into the corner. I tracked them with my peripheral vision, letting my **audio implant auto-adjust, picking up their conversation while filtering out the surrounding noise.**

"You seem pretty cool under pressure," Kaya observed.

Nenah gave a half-shrug. "I've been through worse. But this place… it's different."

Kaya's voice dipped lower. "Do you think we can trust any of these guys?"

Nenah exhaled. "Trust is a luxury we can't afford here. But maybe… we can watch each other's backs."

Kaya considered that. **Heartbeat steadying. Decision made.**

"An alliance? It might be our best shot."

Nenah extended a hand. "Partners?"

Kaya clasped it, firm. "Partners."

A soft vibration against my temple. Karma linked in, her implant syncing with mine for a silent exchange.

Kaya's locking in fast. Nenah's either desperate or calculating.

Kaya's reputation is on the line, I responded mentally. *She needs a win. That makes her dangerous.*

Across the lounge, **Cam Fersk and Zelara Keen** moved through the crowd with **practiced ease. Too smooth. Too intentional.**

I flicked my gaze toward them, **brief eye contact. Click. Connection.**

Their voices slid into my earpiece.

Zelara: *Who do we target first?*

Cam: *Trek and Karma are strong. But Kaya Kellix? She has a reputation to reclaim.*

Zelara: *Nenah Nova's here for personal reasons. Desperation makes people reckless.*

Cam chuckled under his breath. *Let's make it a game within the game—see who can cause the most chaos without getting caught.*

Zelara smirked. *You're on.*

I blinked once. Audio disconnects.

Karma met my eyes, barely tilting her head. She heard it too. **Cam and Zelara were playing their own game.**

Before I could comment, **Zane Astren strode in, voice cutting through the tension like a knife.**

"Alright, contestants! Let's see some enthusiasm before we head to the studio!"

The room stirred. Bodies shifted. The weight of **the game** started to settle in.

Mini-games were set up to distract the players. Holographic puzzles, trivia boards, cultural tests.

Karma and I stood near a trivia screen, its interface pulsing soft blue.

She read aloud, **"How many intelligent species live on Chronoria?"**

I smirked. "Four."

The board flashed: **Correct!**

Nearby, Kaya pieced together a holographic planetary puzzle. Nenah aced a cultural quiz on Old Earth.

"Jazz emerged in the late 19th and early 20th centuries, influenced by African American musical traditions," she said smoothly.

Correct! blinked on her screen.

Cam and Zelara drifted over, their smiles friendly—**but their heart rates slightly accelerated.**

"Hey, Kaya," Zelara said, voice warm, inviting. "I hear you're good at these. Want to join us for a round?"

Kaya hesitated. **Just a fraction of a second. Enough to mean something.**

"Sure, why not?"

Cam turned to Nenah. "What brings you to NexaHunt?"

Nenah's voice dropped. "I'm here to prove myself… and find answers."

Cam and Zelara exchanged a glance. **They'd just found a pressure point to exploit.**

The Studio Unveiling

The NexaHunt theme swelled,

an adventure thrumming through the air as dynamic visuals flooded the studio—

swirling portals, daring explorers, the promise of the unknown.

The Games Narrator's voice echoed through:

"Welcome, adventurers, to the ultimate test of skill, wit, and courage! Prepare yourselves for an epic journey across space and time. Welcome to NexaHunt!"

Scenes of past contestants flickered across the screens—puzzles solved under pressure,

battles fought for dominance, **alien landscapes navigated** with desperation and grit.

"Hosted by the fabulous Lyra Starweaver and Zane Astren, this thrilling adventure will push contestants to their limits. But beware —danger lurks around every corner!"

The crowd roared as Lyra's holographic form appeared, her signature dazzling energy on full display. "Welcome, fellow adventurers! Thank you for joining us on this exhilarating journey across the cosmos!"

Zane Astren stepped forward, flashing his practiced grin. "And I couldn't do this alone! Let's thank our amazing sponsors— Galactic Gear Emporium, Starlight Energy Solutions, Cosmic Cuisine, Universal Travel Agency, and NexaTech!"

Cheers erupted as the **Gatekeepers materialized**, representing the three primary planets.

"Kronos Sun of Chronoria," Lyra announced as a sleek figure stepped forward.

"Sotara Bodhi of Nexotara," a calm, serene presence.

"And Zyna Wave of Zenexis," a ripple of cosmic energy shifting around them.

I hope they don't notice me and Karma.

Then, the moment of truth.

The contestant selection screen flickered to life. Fifty hopefuls. Only a handful would make it.

Lyra's voice rang out: *"Only a handful can compete for glory! Audience, your votes will decide their fate!"*

A countdown appeared—five minutes.

The tension was electric. The studio pulsed with anticipation as names flashed across the screen.

Then, Lyra's voice cut through the noise. *"Time's up! Congratulations to our chosen contestants! Prepare for the adventure of a lifetime!"*

The final selection lit up:

- Seraphin Tynon – Mechanic, mother of two

- Talix Varron – Import/export merchant

- Dario Trek – Interstellar pilot

- Zelara Keen – Social media specialist

- Jorix Renald – Metaphysics engineer

- Nenah Nova – Psychotherapist

- Arista Karma – Physics professor

- Kaya Kellix – Media mogul

- Kai Tanaka – Zen monk

- Cam Fersk – IT specialist

The crowd erupted as we stepped forward, ready.

Lyra grinned. "Contestants, take your places! The NexaHunt adventure begins now!"

And just like that, it was real. The game had begun.

CHAPTER 8
LETS PLAY

LYRA CALLED the names and the Studio lost its mind.

Energy exploded—wild, electric, untamed.

NexaHunt in its purest form.

The crowd was **deafening.** Vibrations hummed through my skin as the chosen contestants moved toward the podiums.

And then there was Zane.

Feeding off the chaos like he **was built for this.**

Waving, whistling, bouncing around like a damn starship launch conductor.

The audience ate it up.

"Get up! Let's hear it for our players!" Zane shouted.

And they did.

Yeah, we love Zane Astren.

Then **Lyra took over.**

Her voice **shifted the energy—smooth, warm, perfectly controlled.**

"Tonight, we welcome some of the finest adventurers across the galaxies, ready to take on the wonders of NexaHunt!"

The words rolled off her tongue, crafted for impact.

The crowd roared.

The air buzzed, thick with **adrenaline.**

Then Zane jumped back in, voice booming.

"That's right, folks! This stellar lineup is about to take on the ultimate challenge! Let's show 'em some love!"

Another eruption of cheers. The kind that rattled your ribs.

Then the first contestants stepped up.

Nenah moved like she owned the damn place.

Slow. Steady. Unshakable.

Her posture? Pure badass.

She hit her spot, standing tall, eyes locked forward.

Locked in. Ready. Dominant.

Rexar moved next.

Dude was *all precision, all calculation.* His eyes flicked across the room, scanning every damn detail like he was memorizing a battlefield.

Calculating. Preparing.

The guy didn't just step into things—**he analyzed them.**

Then Cam.

That spark in his eyes? **Focused. Burning.**

He gave himself a small nod, like a fighter locking in before the first strike. **No hesitation. No second-guessing.**

And then—**me.**

I stepped forward like I **owned the damn place.**

Cocky grin? **Check.**

Smug wink to the audience? **Hell yeah.**

I radiated self-assurance—the kind that either made people love me or want to punch me in the face.

Yeah. **Meathead energy maxed out. Haha ha!**

Seraphin moved in next. She was a whole different breed.

That quiet, controlled walk? **Like a panther stalking the jungle.**

But I knew better.

Her vibe was **wild, untamed—but you wouldn't see it coming until it was too damn late.** She was the type who'd snap in a heartbeat if you pushed the wrong button.

Jorix followed, his expression **flat, unreadable.**

Dude took a slow, deep breath—**centering himself like this was some kind of war strategy.**

"Engage."

Yeah. That was exactly how he saw this. Like the rest of us were just **animals on the board.**

Then Zelara.

She didn't hesitate. **Didn't flinch.** Shoulders squared, gaze locked in.

She wasn't here to play around—**she was locking in. Ready.**

And then—**Kaya.**

Her confidence was effortless.

That little smirk playing on her lips? **Dangerous. Calculated.**

Her gaze flitted around, **already thinking three steps ahead.**

She was here to balance—**to flex just enough, without tipping into arrogance.**

No need to be bossy. **No need to be too scandalous.**

Just the right amount of **sharp.**

The right amount of **dangerous.**

Talix moved next, his expression somewhere between focused and fired up. He gave himself a small nod, **psyching** himself up before taking his place at the podium.

And then—**Karma.**

She approached with a **steady calm,** her energy **quiet but powerful.** She wasn't just here to compete. She was here to **figure out what the hell was really going on.** The **missing contestants.** The **cracks in the game's design.**

Something was **off.** I could tell **she felt it too.**

The **energy in the studio was insane.** Off the charts. The kind of moment you had to **see to believe.** You ever get that feeling? When everything is so intense, so **damn real,** you can't even blink?

Yeah. **It was that.**

The audience felt it too—watching, **holding their breath,** waiting for the first round to begin.

And then something **shifted.**

The **gatekeepers.**

They saw **her. They saw me.** And I knew.

Kronos, the eldest of the three, wrinkled his brow, his gaze lingering **a little too long.** He leaned toward his fellow gate-keepers, murmuring something under his breath. **Sotara** nodded, her face unreadable—**too professional. Too careful.**

Zyna didn't say a word, but his eyes flickered with something else. **Curiosity. Suspicion. Recognition?**

They knew who we were.

I could feel it. The air between us **changed.** The contestants around us? **Oblivious.** But Karma and I weren't just **players in their game.**

We were **a problem.**

(((((O)))))

THE GATEKEEPERS KEPT their expressions neutral.

Composed. Focused.

But I could feel it.

They were watching. Calculating.

Behind them, the portals pulsed, **humming with raw energy.**

Ancient tech. Older than most of the civilizations we knew. And in a few moments, those swirling voids would hurl us across the multiverse.

I stood at my podium, shoulders squared, waiting for the signal.

Most contestants were oblivious.

Or maybe just pretending.

Because the **truth hung over us, like a shadow.**

This was a risk.

Even with all the advancements, all the safety measures, that thought still lingered in the back of your mind:

Will we make it there and back?

I wasn't the only one thinking it.

I saw the glances. The tight grips. The quickened breaths.

Then I caught it—the gatekeepers noticing us.

I shot Karma a quick implant message.

"Dude… I hope they don't blow our cover."

Karma didn't even flinch.

"I'll message Nyx to contact their boss, but… I'm pretty sure the implant is already doing that as we type."

No need to panic. Yet.

The excitement in the Studio hit its peak—electric, suffocating.

Then—Lyra raised her hand.

The entire room shifted.

A hush rippled through the crowd as every set of eyes locked onto her.

"Contestants, prepare yourselves."

Her voice cut through the tension like a blade.

Then, she turned to the audience.

"And now, let's give our contestants a moment of focus… quiet down."

Silence fell.

The moment before the leap.

The **vibe in the room shifted.**

Silence settled over us, thick with anticipation. **You could feel it.** The moment before something big.

Lyra glanced at her cue cards, then lifted her gaze back to us. Steady. Intense.

"Our first question is a crucial one," she said, her voice smooth but commanding. "Contestants, listen carefully."

She paused—**drawing out the tension. Letting it breathe.** She met each of our eyes, one by one.

Then she hit us with it.

"What is the name of the dominant species on that planet? And… what distinguishes them from the others?"

The moment the words left her lips—**BAM.**

Talix **slammed the buzzer.** Fast. **Too fast.**

The studio **stirred**—murmurs rippling through the audience. His confidence was **radiating,** but something wasn't right.

Seconds passed. **Too many.**

Talix didn't speak.

I saw it—the flicker of panic in his eyes. His breathing **hitched.** He was **racking his brain**, but the answer wasn't coming.

The **digital timer** ticked down on the screen, numbers flashing.

Tick. Tick. Tick.

"Time's running out, Talix," Lyra reminded him.

The background **music pulsed low**—steady, insistent. The kind that makes your heartbeat sync up, makes you sweat a little.

"I know—I know this. I'm having a brain fart… ugh!" Talix groaned, his frustration cracking through his voice.

Shit.

He had the speed.

But could he deliver the answer?

Talix let out a huff, his shoulders **sagging, defeated.**

I felt that.

The crowd did too—their disappointment rippled through the room.

Lyra didn't miss a beat.

"Alright, time's up." Her voice cut clean through the tension. **Sharp. Final.**

She tilted her head slightly. **"Talix, do you know the answer?"**

Silence.

"…No?"

Her gaze swept the room.

"Okay, does anyone else care to give it a shot?"

BAM.

Karma hit the buzzer.

I barely moved, but my focus **snapped to her.**

No hesitation. **Not even a second.**

The energy in the room **shifted.**

The audience **stilled.**

Everyone waited.

I knew that look on Karma's face.

I'd seen it before. **The one she wore when she was about to drop something big.**

She let the silence stretch.

Then—**she spoke.**

"This is a trick question. Because the planet has two dominant species."

I caught a few **contestants stiffen.** The audience **murmured.**

Karma? Unbothered. **Completely in control.**

"The first is the Thalorians. Iridescent skin. Telepathic. They keep to themselves."

She let the words settle.

I watched her body language. **Deliberate. Calculated.**

Then she landed the second blow.

"And the others? Humans."

Her tone didn't change. But there was a weight to it now.

"Known for their ingenuity. Their resilience."

She let it breathe.

Then—**her voice sharpened. Just slightly.**

"And for their destructive tendencies."

The air **shifted.**

A collective **gasp.**

I could practically hear the audience's **mental gears grinding.**

I smirked. **She had them.**

Lyra's expression flickered—**something between approval and amusement.**

Then she nodded.

"Well done, Karma… That's correct!"

The **applause thundered.**

Karma barely reacted. **Like she already knew.**

I exhaled, barely moving.

She just **played them.**

And I knew she wasn't done yet.

The first question was down.

And the game? Officially on.

The studio **buzzed—alive, electric.**

Karma stepped off to the waiting area near the roulette table. She didn't look back—**locked in, ready.**

I stayed. **Breathing steady. Mind sharper than ever.**

Lyra's voice cut through the hum of anticipation.

"Alright, contestants, here comes the second question. Get ready!"

The **lights dimmed.**

Not much—just enough to make every set of eyes snap to the center of the room—to Lyra.

Her **shimmering hologram flickered as she read.**

"Question two: How many moons does the planet Earth have?"

The words **hung.**

With a flick of her wrist, the question **flashed onto the giant screens.**

Behind her, a **rotating image of Earth.** A single moon.

A visual cue. A setup.

Didn't matter. Because I already knew.

BAM.

My hand slammed the buzzer.

The **room froze.**

A beat.

Then—**the countdown clock ticked.**

Tick. Tick. Tick.

The sound stretched the moment.

Lyra's eyes locked onto mine.

No hesitation. **No second-guessing.** I held her gaze. Didn't blink.

"The planet Earth has only one moon."

My **voice—steady. Absolute.**

The crowd held their breath.

I knew I was right.

The only question was—

Would the game agree?

Lyra's **smile widened** as she nodded. "That's correct, Trek! Well done!"

The **crowd erupted.** Cheers, applause—a mix of admiration and relief. They loved **a quick, clean win.**

I grinned, soaking it in. "Can we do another question? That was too easy."

I shot **Kaya a wink.** She just *smirked, nodding slightly*—approval without words.

The crowd **laughed, the tension breaking.**

"Trek, please," Lyra said, gesturing toward the waiting area. "You've earned your spot at the roulette table. Head over and get ready for the next phase."

The **spotlight followed me** as I moved, locking in on my confident stride.

I made my way to the designated **waiting area**—a semi-circular coral lined with plush seats and a transparent barrier. From here, I had a clear view of the studio floor and everything happening in the game.

Karma was already there. I held up a hand, and we met in a **sharp, satisfying high-five.**

"Nice job out there," she said, her grin easy, encouraging.

I matched her smile. This was the kind of camaraderie that made the game worth playing.

But I wasn't just soaking in the moment.

As I turned my gaze toward the audience, **I studied the host.**

The **gatekeepers.**

Dressed in **monk-like outfits with glowing accents,** they stood by the portal, **stoic, unreadable.**

Watching.

I took note.

Because something told me **this game wasn't just about answering questions.**

Lyra's holographic form hovered at the center of the stage, her presence **commanding even in silence.**

The vibe in the studio was electric. The audience's eyes flickered between the contestants and the **giant screens**, anticipation thick in the air.

From my spot in the **waiting area,** I shifted my gaze back to the contestants still at their podiums. **Their expressions said it all.**

Some looked **anxious.** Others, **determined.**

No doubt—**the competition was heating up.** Every answer mattered now.

I leaned back in my seat, the rush of adrenaline still **thrumming through me.** The **next phase** was coming, and I was **ready for it.**

Lyra straightened slightly, preparing to ask the **third question.**

Her voice sliced through the tension like a blade.

"Contestants, are you ready for the next challenge?"

The crowd **leaned in.**

Eyes locked. **No distractions. No noise.**

Lyra's holographic display flickered as she spoke.

"Question number three: Describe the planet's technology level compared to Earth… and what advancements or innovations are unique to their world."

The **buzzers lit up.**

Contestants tensed, their minds **racing.**

Five seconds passed. Nothing.

Then—a spark.

Kai Tanaka's eyes lit up. A flicker of understanding.

BAM.

His hand slammed the buzzer, his movement **sharp, decisive.**

He was ready.

Time stretched.

The countdown clock **ticked away,** each second dragging like an eternity.

Kai Tanaka was locked in. His face **tight with concentration,** his mind **racing** to recall everything from the orientation.

Seconds left.

Then—**something clicked.**

A spark of realization flashed across his face, and he **blurted out his answer in a rush.**

"Our planet's technology is far more advanced than Earth's! We have portal technology, anti-gravity transportation, and holographic communication. Their tech is constantly being refined and improved."

The moment he finished, the tension in the studio **snapped.**

The audience let out a collective sigh of relief, the heavy anticipation **melting away.**

He had cut it close, but he made it.

"That's correct! Great job, Tanaka," Lyra said, her voice warm with approval. "And now, let's add some excitement!"

Before anyone could react, Zane burst onto the stage, his energy lighting up the room.

"Let's hear it for Kai Tanaka, everyone!" He threw his arms wide, leading the audience into applause.

The cheers **boomed,** but Zane wasn't done.

"But we're not stopping there! It's time for an audience bonus question!"

Above the crowd, a holographic interface flickered to life, scanning for a participant. Lights danced over the rows of spectators.

Then—the spotlight stopped.

It landed on a young woman in the third row. Her face was a mix of thrill and nerves.

Zane's grin widened. "Alright! What's your name?"

Her voice barely made it over the crowd.

"Maria."

"Okay, Maria, here's your chance to win a prize. Ready?" Zane's voice boomed, the crowd **buzzing with anticipation.**

Maria nodded, her eyes wide.

"Here's your question," Zane said, his tone **teasing but encouraging.** "What year did the first human set foot on the Moon?"

Maria's face **lit up. "1969!"** she shouted confidently.

"That's correct!" Zane yelled, and the **studio erupted in applause.**

"Maria, you've just won a brand-new holo-communicator! Congratulations!"

She **beamed**, the audience cheering for her.

Zane turned back to the contestants, flashing his signature grin. "But now, back to our main event. Kai, you've earned your spot in the waiting area. Join the others and get ready for the next phase."

Kai strolled toward the waiting area, flashing the audience a confident smile before **high-fiving Zane.**

But just as he reached his seat—

Zane held up a hand. "Wait a second, Kai! How about another challenge for you, too?"

Kai **paused.** Intrigued.

Zane smirked, turning to the audience. "One more question, just for fun!"

The crowd leaned in, hungry for more.

"What's the name of the largest volcano in the Earthling's solar system?"

Kai's brow furrowed. **Thinking.**

Then—*a spark of recognition.*

"Um… Olympus Mons on Mars?" he guessed.

Zane grinned. "You got it right! But unfortunately, that one doesn't count toward your score. Great job, though!"

The crowd **applauded** as Kai finally took his place in the waiting area, ready for the next challenge.

I glanced at the **remaining contestants.** A few exchanged **nervous looks.** Their turn was **coming fast.**

Lyra's voice carried effortlessly across the studio. "Are there any restrictions or taboos you should be aware of when interacting with Earthlings?"

The *contestants leaned in.*

I kept my focus sharp, my attention locked on the smallest reactions. Every shift in body language. Every hesitation. **All of it mattered.**

Then—**a sharp movement.**

With a **quick flick of her wrist, Seraphin Tynon** slammed the **buzzer first.**

Her **eyes burned with determination.**

"Yes," she declared, her voice slicing through the tension. "Contestants should avoid making direct eye contact with the indigenous species. It's considered a sign of aggression."

Silence stretched.

Lyra took her time—**just a few extra seconds.**

Playing with the moment.

This was *NexaHunt, after all.* Drama was part of the game.

Her fingers toyed with the answer card.

Then, with a smirk and a mischievous twinkle in her eye, she asked, "Are you sure that's your final answer?"

The room **held its breath.**

And Seraphin? She was about to find out just how much Nexa-Hunt loved to make its players sweat.

"I mean... yeah."

Seraphin's voice **wavered.** She glanced around, suddenly **not so sure.**

A ripple of whispers moved through the crowd.

Then—Lyra nodded, a small smirk tugging at her lips.

"That's correct! Well done, Seraphin!"

The **studio erupted.**

Cheers. Applause. The kind that **shakes the walls.**

Seraphin's **chest swelled with pride.** She owned that win.

The momentum? **Hers now.**

I felt **movement beside me.**

Karma.

We didn't say a word. **Didn't have to.**

For just a second, our **eyes met.**

A silent exchange.

We both knew.

The **gatekeepers were watching.**

Even in the middle of this **high-energy spectacle,** their eyes hadn't strayed.

Neither had ours.

I exhaled, shifting my focus **back to the game.**

Just as **Zane jumped in.**

"Let's hear it for Seraphin, everyone!" His voice boomed, igniting another wave of excitement.

Then—his **signature smirk.** That look that meant he was about to throw a curveball.

"But hold on, folks! We've got a special treat! An audience member is about to get a shot at a prize."

The **crowd buzzed.**

Zane **scanned the room.** Then—**locked in.**

"Alright, you there in the blue shirt! Come on down!"

A young guy shot up, **grinning, nervous.** He weaved through the rows, stepping onto the stage like he was walking on a dream.

Zane **handed him the mic.**

"What's your name?"

"Logan." He steadied his voice.

Zane's **grin widened.**

"Alright, Logan… here's your question for a chance to win a limited edition NexaHunt merch pack."

A pause. Then, in a **playfully challenging tone.**

"What is the capital city of the planet Chronoria?"

The room **stilled.**

All eyes were on **Logan.**

But my mind? **Still partially locked on the gatekeepers.**

Because this wasn't just a game.

And Karma and I weren't just players.

Logan took a beat, then answered confidently.

"Zalora."

QUIET NOW.

Zane tilted his head, grinning.

"Ooh, so close, Logan! The correct answer is Celestara. But great try! Thanks for playing!"

The **audience clapped, cheered.**

Logan **shrugged, still smiling** as he made his way back to his seat—a good sport, despite the miss.

Zane turned back toward us, energy never dipping.

He met Seraphin's hand in a **quick high-five, ushering her to the roulette waiting area.**

"Let's keep this energy up! Next question coming right up!"

The studio **buzzed.**

Chatter between contestants was louder than in past episodes.

Competition was heating up.

Not that it fazed me. *Or Karma.*

We were locked in. Watching. Taking note.

Lyra let the **tension hang.**

Then her voice **sliced through the noise.**

"One of you should know this next answer. It should be easy for one of you."

She let the words linger. **Dangling like bait.**

A challenge. A tease.

The **audience leaned forward.**

Faces lit with anticipation.

Zane played into it, pacing the stage, high-fiving audience members.

Keeping the energy **electric.**

But among the contestants?

Tension thickened.

Some were anxious.

Waiting.

Ready to **strike** when the next question dropped.

Lyra knew **exactly** what she was doing.

And so did we.

Karma and I exchanged a look.

A flicker of **amusement. Of knowing.**

She was playing with their minds.

But that wouldn't work on us.

"Name … Name one of the endangered species that inhabit Earth."

Lyra's voice was smooth, deliberate. She **paused, letting the words settle,** her eyes drifting over the audience and contestants.

She was savoring this moment.

Zelara **didn't hesitate.**

Her hand slammed the buzzer so fast it was **almost a blur.**

"Blue-throated Macaw." She held her breath, waiting for Lyra's confirmation. Her heartbeat pounded in her ears, locking her into the moment.

Determined. Focused. Unshakable.

On the **massive displays**, the faces of the other contestants flickered into view.

Their expressions? A wild mix of eagerness, tension, and, in some cases… pure chaos.

But Zelara wasn't looking at them.

She was **locked in.**

Lyra let the tension stretch.

Then—"Yes, yes, yes!" Zelara burst out, her voice triumphant.

The relief was instant. A radiant smile spread across her face.

"Is that your final answer, Zelara?" Lyra's voice dipped, teasing. Holding onto the suspense.

Zelara's chin lifted. "Yes. That's my final answer."

Lyra nodded.

"That's correct, Zelara! Well done!"

The audience **erupted.** The sound hit the walls, bounced back, and filled the studio.

Zelara basked in it, soaking up her victory.

Then **Zane appeared, grinning.** He met her hand with a **sharp high-five** before leading her toward the **waiting area.**

The game was picking up speed.

And I could feel it—the shift.

Another step closer to whatever was waiting for us.

"Let's give it up for Zelara, everyone!"

Zane's voice boomed through the studio, electric with energy.

The crowd followed his lead, a wave of cheers crashing through the arena.

Zelara took her place in the corral, exchanging nods with the other contestants.

Confidence unshakable.

The game wasn't slowing down.

Every question, every answer—the stakes climbed higher.

Lyra **lifted her gaze,** voice smooth but commanding.

"Okay, now… are you ready for the next question?"

The audience **erupted.**

Their energy spiked, deafening.

Then—Lyra's voice sliced through the noise.

"Are there any rules or taboos for contestants… when they interact with the planet's inhabitants? If so, name one taboo."

The moment the words left her lips—

BAM.

Kaya hit the buzzer. Like **lightning.**

The **studio exploded.** "Kaya! Kaya! Kaya!"

The crowd chanted her name, their voices **booming in perfect sync.**

She **thrived on it.**

A confident grin spread across her face.

Her **eyes locked on Lyra.**

"Yes," she said, voice sharp, certain. "Contestants should avoid being aggressive. They should also avoid disrespecting the planet's inhabitants' customs."

Lyra's **smile widened.**

Approval clear.

"That's correct, Kaya!"

The **crowd erupted again.**

Then—Lyra tilted her head, a playful glint in her eyes.

"Well done! Now then… do you know the second part?"

From the sidelines, **I watched Kaya.**

Something about her **nagged at me.** A weird pull—**familiar, yet not.**

We'd never crossed paths in our usual circles. But **her face, her energy… it struck a chord.**

I caught myself **smirking. Intrigued.**

Kaya? **Completely unbothered.**

She stood firm, delivering her answer without hesitation.

"One taboo on the planet is never making direct eye contact with the elders of the dominant species," she stated smoothly. "It's considered highly disrespectful and can result in severe consequences—like imprisonment or expulsion."

The words **hung.**

Lyra **paused.** Dragging out the tension like always.

The audience held their breath.

Kaya? **Unshaken.** Her stance—solid. Confidence unwavering.

Meanwhile, Zane, ever the showman, took his chance.

"Hey, everyone! Let's see how well you know your intergalactic etiquette!" His voice boomed. "Who here can tell me another taboo?"

Hands shot up.

He scanned the crowd and pointed to a young woman in the front row.

"Never touch their sacred artifacts without permission!" she blurted.

A **huge grin** stretched across her face.

"That's a good one!" Zane tossed her a prize. "Keep those answers coming!"

Back on stage, Lyra finally spoke.

Her voice **burst with enthusiasm.**

"That's correct, Kaya!"

The crowd roared. And me? I kept my eyes on Kaya.

Because something about her still didn't sit right.

Kaya basked in the moment.

The crowd's cheers fueled her, their energy feeding into the fire that was already burning inside her.

With each correct answer, she edged closer to her goal. Closer to proving herself on an intergalactic stage.

Zane strode over, grinning. He met her hand with an encouraging high-five before motioning her toward the **corral area.**

I watched as she walked away.

Something about her **kept pulling at me.**

She wasn't just another competitor.

I didn't know why, but I needed to figure it out.

The other contestants felt it too.

The competition was shifting.

Kaya's confidence was **contagious.** Her success added weight to the game.

The vibe in the studio hadn't changed.

Still electric. Still charged.

Lyra stepped forward, ready to keep things moving.

"Contestants, we're moving on to the next question."

Her voice **resonated with control,** with authority.

The audience was still locked in. Their energy never dipped— if anything, it climbed.

And Zane?

He knew exactly how to keep it soaring.

"Who's ready for the next challenge?" He called out, **his voice booming.** "Let's hear it for our contestants!"

A deafening roar erupted.

Then I turned my attention back to the stage.

Jorix. Nenah. Talix. Cam.

The **final four** left in the first round.

I studied their faces.

Anxious. Tense.

Except for Nenah. She was calm. Too calm.

The audience noticed it too.

A question hung in the air—what's her game plan?

Is she about to make a move no one sees coming?

"Alright, contestants, let's keep this momentum going! Here's your next question."

The audience hushed.

The shift was **instant.**

I could feel the weight of it—the thick tension pressing down.

Lyra's **eyes gleamed** as she delivered the next challenge.

"What primary export or resource is planet Earth known for? Also… is it a known or unknown resource for the planet's inhabitants?"

A murmur rippled through the studio.

I watched the contestants—**fingers hovering, pulses ticking.**

Then—**Talix struck.**

His hand slammed the buzzer.

A **grin spread across his face.** Confident. Unshaken.

Zane jumped in, amping up the moment. "You've got 30 seconds, Talix. Come on, I know you want to play this game!"

Talix **took a slow breath.**

Then his voice cut through the silence.

"Earth's primary export? Human labor."

The crowd rippled with murmurs.

Lyra's brows shot up, but she kept her cool, giving him a nod to continue.

Talix did. **Unapologetic. Unflinching.**

"Additionally… abductions by the Grey aliens for export are known by some," he added. "Yet, whether it's known or unknown is still up for debate among Earth's inhabitants."

A wave of stunned silence followed.

Even I felt it. Because Talix? He wasn't wrong.

As Talix headed to the waiting area, Zane, never missing a beat, fired up the crowd.

"Who's ready for more surprises? This game is just heating up!"

The audience **roared.**

Meanwhile, the remaining contestants shifted.

I could see it—the way their shoulders tensed, the way they exchanged wary glances.

They knew.

Their turn was coming.

The air was thick with anticipation. Each of them was bracing for impact.

Except for Nenah.

She remained **calm. Unshaken.**

Her gaze flicked to Talix as he passed, giving him a **small nod.**

Encouraging. Steady.

Talix, despite his **near miss,** squared his shoulders.

I could see it—the determination sparking in his eyes.

He had **made an impact.** That much was clear.

And now? He was ready to push forward.

Lyra's gaze swept over the remaining contestants, her expression a mix of challenge and encouragement.

"Get ready, everyone. The next question is coming up, and it's going to test your knowledge—and your nerve."

The studio lights dimmed slightly.

A subtle shift. A layer of drama added to the moment.

This game was **far from over.**

And every single question could flip everything.

I exhaled, watching as the tension in the room **thickened.**

Then—Lyra's voice cut through the silence.

A hint of **drama in her tone.**

"And then there were three."

A **playful smirk** tugged at her lips.

Her gaze locked onto the last ones standing.

Nenah. Jorix. Cam.

Each of them stood poised, ready.

Ready to play.

Lyra soaked in the energy, feeding off the crowd's wild excitement.

"How's everyone enjoying the game so far?"

The **studio exploded** with cheers; the sound reverberating off every surface.

I didn't join in, but **I felt it.**

This wasn't just a game anymore. Not for me. Not for Karma.

As the crowd **settled,** Lyra's voice dropped into that smooth, suspenseful tone.

"Now, for our final three contestants, here's question eight."

A pause.

A perfectly timed breath of tension.

"What can players buy with the local currency, and where can they find vendors or markets to spend it?"

I watched **Jorix, Nenah, and Cam.**

No one moved.

Not at first.

Then—Cam struck.

His hand hit the buzzer fast, his grin wide.

Confident.

Too confident?

The room **hovered on edge.**

Then, Cam's voice cut through the silence.

"Contestants can use the local currency to buy a wide array of goods—from rare artifacts to essential supplies. The Federation-approved vendors can be located using the wrist-comm device. It guides you to various markets and stalls throughout the planet."

I exhaled, flicking a glance at **Karma.**

She barely moved, but I saw it—the slight shift, the way her fingers flexed.

She caught it too.

Lyra's eyes flickered with approval.

"That is correct, Cam Fersk! Well done!"

The crowd erupted again.

Cam **soaked it in.**

But I wasn't watching him anymore.

I was watching the shift in the game.

Because something told me—we weren't just playing anymore.

Lyra let the moment stretch, milking the tension.

"How's everyone enjoying the game so far?"

The **crowd roared.** The energy rushed through the studio like a wave.

I didn't react, but **I felt it.**

This wasn't just a game. Not to me. Not to Karma.

I shifted slightly, my gaze locking onto the final three.

Jorix. Nenah. Cam.

They didn't see it yet.

But I did.

Something was **building under the surface.**

As the **cheers faded,** Lyra's voice dropped, smooth but sharp.

"Now, for our final three contestants, here's question eight."

A **pause.** The kind that **presses against your chest.**

"What can players buy with the local currency, and where can they find vendors or markets to spend it?"

A **beat.** Then—Cam moved first.

His hand slammed the *buzzer.*

"Contestants can use the local currency to buy a wide array of goods—from rare artifacts to essential supplies. The Federation-approved vendors can be located using the wrist-comm device."

I exhaled slowly. Too perfect.

I glanced at Karma.

She **caught it too.**

Lyra's eyes flickered with approval.

"That is correct, Cam! Well done!"

The **crowd exploded.**

Cam soaked it in.

But **I wasn't watching him.** I was watching **the shift.**

Because something told me—we weren't just playing anymore.

"Correct! Now, tell us—how do we know about this planet, Earth? You have 30 seconds."

Lyra's words **hung in the air.**

A bonus question. A test.

I watched as Nenah's mind raced.

She wasn't rushing, though.

I could see it—the gears turning, the pieces locking into place.

The timer ticked down.

Then—clarity.

Her voice cut through the quiet.

"All three sister planets should never forget the catastrophic event from 80 years ago. It brought our civilizations to the brink of collapse. If it weren't for the Galactic Federation informing us of the source… a parallel universe and its destructive nature—the planet Earth and its atomic detonations… we wouldn't have advanced at the rate we have."

Silence.

Heavy.

Weighted.

The **room shifted.**

Nenah's words **hit hard.**

Not just for the contestants. Not just for the audience. For **everyone.**

I felt it too.

The way the truth pressed down.

Nenah hadn't just answered a question. She'd reminded the universe of its scars.

Lyra took her time.

Holding the moment.

Then—her voice rang out.

"You are right!"

The studio **erupted.**

Cheers. Relief. Smiles spread through the crowd.

But I wasn't looking at them.

I was watching **Nenah.**

She didn't smile.

Not really.

Her answer had been fact. Truth. A reminder.

And I had a feeling she knew it was more than that.

Lyra's voice **sliced through the noise.**

"And now, we'll take a brief sponsor break before the final round."

The lights dimmed.

The audience settled.

The anticipation? **Still thick.**

This wasn't just the end of a round. This was a shift. A turning point.

And we were about to step into the unknown.

CHAPTER 9
ROULETTE

MOVING from the corral felt like stepping into a pressure cooker. The Roulette phase loomed ahead, and **the tension buzzed through my skin like static.**

Every contestant carried their own brand of anxiety, but hell, it felt personal, like the air itself was pushing against my chest.

Excitement and dread warred inside me. The questions had been tough, but this next phase? Wildcard territory. My mind spun with possibilities.

What if the wheel lands on something brutal? What if Karma and I get separated?

I forced myself to breathe, to stay sharp. No way I was letting uncertainty eat me alive. I glanced at Karma—steady, collected. Did she feel the same gnawing under the surface, or was she just better at masking it?

Nenah stayed close to Kaya, the two of them sharing this soft, almost invisible tether. I caught the way Nenah squeezed Kaya's hand, still hanging onto the fleeting reassurance. **They looked solid. Strong. But Roulette was a beast that didn't care how close you were.**

Aria, poor thing, wore her doubt like a shroud. I didn't need to hear her thoughts to know she was stuck replaying past mistakes, paralyzed by the idea of screwing up again. Rexar was trying to prop her up, but fear had a way of sinking its teeth in and not letting go.

Then there was Wei Chen—the new guy. All logic, all calculation. I could almost feel the heat radiating off his mind as he ran scenarios in real-time. **He was a thinker. Dangerous in the right—or wrong—situation.** I clocked the tension between him and Jorix. Shaky alliances were blood in the water here.

The studio crackled with a different energy now—the audience was back, hungry for chaos. Whispers floated over the hum of machinery and lights.

"Did you see Trek's face? He's hiding something."

"Nenah and Kaya look strong, but Roulette's a bitch."

Up on the live feeds, viewers across the galaxy threw their opinions into the roaring void of social media. Polls flashed and hashtags exploded, whipping the crowd into a frenzy.

Lyra's voice, syrupy and sharp, cut through the madness: "Who do you think will come out on top? Don't be shy—let's hear it!"

The crowd went feral. Glow sticks waved like neon spears. Lyra soaked it all in, practically *feeding* on the energy.

The big screen behind her flared to life with live polls—Karma and I were leading by a hair.

Good. Let them think they know who's got the edge. Let them get cocky.

Lyra flashed a grin, voice playful but with an undercurrent of menace. "It looks like Trek and Karma are leading the votes, but anything can happen in the Roulette phase. Keep those votes coming—your participation could make all the difference!"

Across from me, Karma mirrored my stance at the roulette table, cool as a glacier. We were playing our roles to perfection: Calm. Unshakeable. But underneath? **Every cell in my body was locked in a dead sprint.**

Lyra's voice snapped the studio back to attention. "It's time for the partner selection round. This is where fate and luck start dictating your futures!"

The spotlight shifted—harsh, hot, making the sweat bead at the base of my neck.

Lyra's voice rang out again, "Please welcome Trek, Nenah, Talix, Seraphin, and Rexar!"

The room detonated with cheers, the energy slamming into me like a wall of sound.

The wheel started to spin. Vibrant, hypnotic. I leaned in, watching it blur into a spectrum of risk and reward.

Nenah stepped up first. She radiated this badass calm, like the earlier wins had stitched steel into her spine. Lucky her. **The die felt heavy in her hand, weighted with every possible future.**

She rolled. The triangular die clattered and landed with a glowing "1." Simple choice ahead. Five boxes flickered into view on the overhead screen. I held my breath as she picked one with a casual nod.

Zane tapped it open—Cosmic Cuisine for a year. Cute prize. Crowd went nuts.

But it wasn't over. The six-sided die tumbled next, flashing green. Bonus round. Nenah didn't flinch. Lyra, practically vibrating with excitement, threw the question out:

"What event in 1947 sparked global interest and speculation?"

The air thickened. Nenah didn't miss a beat. "The Roswell UFO crash."

The studio blew up in cheers. Correct.

Lyra, grinning like the cat that caught the canary, leaned in closer. "For a chance to quadruple your points—What's the connection between the three sister planets and the 1947 atomic blast on Earth?"

I caught the split-second glance Nenah shot me.

Was that a signal? A warning? A flex?

I filed it away.

Nenah answered—clear, composed, way too knowledgeable for coincidence. The silence that followed was heavy with realization.

When the die finally revealed a zero—instant portal access— the place lost its damn mind.

Something's not right with her. The thought burned in my gut. **She's connected to Mara somehow. I can feel it.**

Nenah didn't hesitate. "I choose Kaya."

Of course you do. The ex of our dear Mara.

Karma caught my look and nodded slightly. We both knew— we were swimming in deeper waters than we realized.

AI avatars of Nenah and Kaya flashed across the monitors, locked in a digital battle-dance.

Zane beckoned Nenah to the portal. Lyra's voice carried over the roar of the crowd: "Congratulations to our first pair, Nenah and Kaya!"

As they crossed into the unknown, I squared my shoulders. **My turn.**

I swaggered to the roulette table like I had the whole damn world in my pocket. Couldn't let them see the truth—the calculations running like wildfire in my head. Had to keep it light. Playful. A show.

Zane shot me a grin. I matched it, tossing a wink just for good measure.

The crowd lapped it up, the energy slamming into me in waves. Lyra watched, amused, but sharp—always sharp.

The dice felt cool in my palm. Heavy. **Like holding a loaded weapon you couldn't fully control.**

I gave them an exaggerated flick, letting them tumble across the velvet with a satisfying clatter. I flashed Karma a grin mid-roll, cocky as hell. Gotta keep up appearances. **Stay loose. Stay lethal.**

The four-sided die landed first.

Twenty. **Boom. Final pair secured.**

I felt the audience's roar rise, feeding the heat under my skin. Good. Let them cheer. Let them *think* I was just another cocky contestant. **Invisibility through arrogance. My favorite damn magic trick.**

I caught a flicker across Karma's face—concern. Barely there, but I caught it.

Yeah, I'm playing it risky. But it's a calculated risk. Trust me.

The six-sided die spun. Slowed.

Landed on three.

The screens on every seat lit up like a field of stars, roulette-style.

Interactive questions. **Of course. Let's make it spicy.**

The game narrator's voice floated above the din:

"In your opinion, which countries and societies on Earth show the most advanced capabilities and offer hope for the future? Provide one correct answer."

For a heartbeat, my mind blanked.

Shit. Focus.

The audience held their breath, their silence crushing against my eardrums.

Then—clarity.

I let a smirk curl my lips as I leaned into the mic.

"The countries that prioritize science, the environment, and social equality. Like Norway—with their renewable energy moves—and Japan, tech-savvy and resilient as hell. And China too—can't forget their advancements."

Boom. Delivered.

The studio exploded. Cheers bounced off the walls like ricochets.

I shot another wink at Zane.

Yeah, I'm a damn smart cookie. Bet you didn't see that coming.

Lyra's small, impressed smile didn't go unnoticed either.

"Looks like our charming contestant might have a chance after all," she mused aloud.

Karma, though... her stare could've burned a hole through my skull.

Ease up, Karma. I know the stakes. I'm not about to blow this now.

The results finalized.

Trek and Karma—confirmed. Last portal pair.

The music shifted again, that trance-like hum rippling through the studio. Monitors lit up, splashing our AI-animated avatars across the massive screens—locked in, ready, waiting.

Zane and Lyra did a quick celebratory dance, feeding the fire in the room. Then Zane gestured for us to follow, where the Gatekeepers stood stoic by the portal controls.

Lyra's voice lifted above the noise:

"Congratulations to our final pair, Trek and Karma!"

The studio's roar swallowed me whole. But beneath the adrenaline, my mind stayed razor sharp.

This wasn't just a game anymore. Every step forward was another move on the board. Another chance to win—or lose it all.

We moved into the low-lit corral again, that dark cocoon away from the main studio.

The energy shifted, quieter, more dangerous.

Kaya sidled up, her movements careful, guarded.

"You know," she said, just above a whisper, "I didn't join this for the prize money."

I raised an eyebrow.

Oh? This oughta be good.

She hesitated, glancing around before locking eyes with me.

"Mara," she breathed. **The name dropped like a weight between us.**

"He's done things, Trek. Bad things. This game... it's my only shot at getting close enough to expose him."

I studied her. **The fire in her voice mirrored something deep inside me.**

Different motives. Same war.

"You think this game'll really give you that shot?" I asked.

"It has to," she said. "And... we need to stick together. Watch each other's backs."

I nodded once. **Solidarity forged in shared danger.**

"Alright. But if it comes down to it..."

She smiled, faint but fierce.

"May the best player win."

We clasped hands briefly—an agreement.

And as I pulled her close, I slipped the tracker into her pack, seamless.

Activated it with a silent command from my comm. device.

Had to keep options open. Always.

The timer blared, a war drum pounding against my ribs.

The portal phase was beginning.

Lyra's voice, crisp as a blade, called out:

"Ladies and gentlemen, we have one last interactive play before we conclude this phase!"

I tensed, ready for anything.

The roulette wheel spun—harder, faster.

Shock rippled through the room when Seraphin was eliminated—Wei Chen taking her place.

Wei Chen.

Now that's a wild card if I ever saw one.

His bio scrolled on the screens—brilliant engineer from Zenexis.

Yeah, buddy, you're gonna change the game. One way or another.

Lyra's voice practically purred with excitement.

"Stay tuned, folks. The journey's just beginning."

No kidding.

The final portal entry order unfurled before us like a battle plan.

Nenah and Kaya stepped up first, hand in hand, disappearing into the swirling energy without hesitation.

Respect.

Rexar and Aria followed next. Rexar solid as a mountain; Aria —tentative, but moving.

Then Talix and Jax. Then Wei and Jorix—New Orleans their destination.

The room's tension coiled tighter with each jump.

Finally—us.

Lyra turned toward us, voice gleaming with anticipation:

"Trek, Karma. It's your moment now."

I flashed the audience a rakish grin.

"Been a pleasure, folks. Don't blink—you'll miss the good part."

Countdown started.

No second thoughts. No backing down.

Karma's voice cut through like a steel blade:

"Not a chance. I've been waiting for this moment my whole life."

We locked eyes. Stepped forward.

Together.

The portal's swirling light swallowed us whole.

And my last thought before the world warped and twisted out of shape:

This is it. No more hiding. No more games. Time to bring the real fight.

CHAPTER 10
WRONG CITY

THE PORTAL SPIT us out into a narrow alley, wrapped in shadows and the buzz of flickering light.

A low hum hung in the air—**wet pavement, burnt oil, and something sharp and sweet, like ginger and firecrackers.**

Mandarin echoed off the brick walls in fast bursts, layered over the clatter of dishes and muffled basslines bleeding from nearby storefronts. **San Francisco. Not New Orleans.**

Karma didn't have to say it. I felt it in the shift of her posture, the way her hand tightened around the comm.

"We're in the wrong city," she muttered, teeth clenched behind the words.

Not the wrong world. Just **a few thousand miles** off the mark. Might as well have been a different planet.

She flicked on the comm, scanning for a signal, trying to untangle scraps of local chatter bleeding in from the street. I caught the scent of grilled meat and sugar glaze from a vendor stall just beyond the alley mouth. Chinatown.

This wasn't just a misfire. This was a problem.

I exhaled slow, steady. Frustration buzzed under my skin like a glitch in the interface. "Stay focused," I told her—and myself. "Mara's secrets aren't gonna uncover themselves, and we're not bailing till we drag them into the light."

The comm crackled. Nyx's voice cut in, cool and detached. "Last-minute change. Stand by. Familiarize yourselves with the area. Updated logistics en route."

"Understood," Karma replied, already moving.

We stepped out of the alley and into the pulse of the city. Lanterns swung overhead, painting the street in bruised reds and gold. *The sizzle of food, the slap of shoes on wet concrete, the thrum of too many lives stacked too close together*—it all hit at once.

Beautiful chaos.

Wrong city. Wrong setup. Same mission.

"You heard the boss," I said, eyes scanning everything. "Let's mingle."

Stay alert. Stay ready. No time for the jet lag.

We moved through the crowded streets, shoulders brushing against strangers, every step sinking us deeper into the chaos. The city buzzed with energy—honking cars, various light reflections in puddles, a thousand conversations overlapping like tangled code. Karma and I did our best to blend in, but let's be real—we stood out. Hard. **Two off-worlders dressed like they walked out of an ops sim, surrounded by Earthlings who barely glanced up from their screens or soy noodles.**

The comm dinged. Nyx. A location dropped on the display— rendezvous coordinates and a name.

I caught Karma's eye. "Let's go. We've got a contact," she said, already turning toward the route. "Might be someone who can actually help us."

The address took us deeper into Chinatown. Our contact? Posted up in a Chinese restaurant. Karma lit up before we even stepped inside.

Of course she did. Foodie to the core. One of her favorite things back home was trying new food—especially Earth stuff. For her, eating good in another world? That was the real adventure.

The moment we walked through the door, the scent hit like a warm punch—ginger, garlic, sweet soy, sizzling oil. My stomach rumbled on instinct. Karma? Grinning like she'd just walked into paradise.

Yeah. That girl was hungry.

The place was loud—chatter bouncing off wood-paneled walls, kitchen flames roaring in the back, glassware clinking like wind chimes in a storm. There was something familiar about the vibe. Not the decor, not even the smell—**but the energy.**

It felt like NOLA. One of our favorite haunts. Same rhythm. Same kind of noise. Same kind of soul.

I scanned the crowd while Karma soaked it all in. First meal on Earth? She wasn't just ready—**she was glowing.**

But me? I couldn't fully relax. Not with Mara still out there. Not with this contact still unseen.

Eyes open. Play it cool. Let Karma enjoy the moment, but stay sharp.

This city was beautiful. But underneath it, something stank.

"Excuse me, your table is ready," a soft voice floated from behind us.

We turned—and there she was. Young, poised, wrapped in a velvet dress the color of midnight. Light blue and white flowers bloomed across the fabric like they were painted by hand. She looked like she belonged to another era.

"Oh! I'm sorry," Karma said, quick with the charm, flashing her a warm smile. Always smooth. The hostess nodded, then turned and led us through a maze of tightly packed tables and elbow-close conversations.

Every step felt like it pulled us deeper. Closer to something. Answers, maybe. If we were lucky.

She stopped at a booth tucked near the back, just shy of the kitchen swing doors. "Here's your table. Enjoy your meal." Then she was gone.

Finally.

A sliver of time to breathe. To talk. To plan.

We slid into the booth—backs to the wall, eyes on the room. The sounds wrapped around us—clinking glassware, plates hitting wood, the sharp hiss of woks working overtime. Nobody paid us any mind. **Perfect cover.**

Karma scanned the restaurant with that quiet curiosity she always carried. I tapped into the datapad, running queries and pulling fragments from our source logs. **Static.** Layers of fragmented intel. But something was here.

"Our sources show the last known player from Season One came here. This exact place," I said, keeping my voice low. "We need to find someone who might know what happened to him. Anything they've got—we take it."

"Oh, yeah…" Karma leaned in, voice steady but edged. "You know how it is. Seeking answers on this world? It's never straightforward. But if our contact's solid, we'll have something to work with."

I glanced toward the front. Still no one approaching. "About them—how are we supposed to know who they are?"

She looked at me, cool as ever. "Nyx said they'll know us."

I raised a brow. **Vague much?**

"So we sit," she said, settling back. "And we wait. They'll find us."

Great. No pressure. Just trust the mystery contact on a planet where everyone stares too long and says too little.

But we didn't have a better lead.

So yeah—we sat. Waited. Let the noise wrap around us like smoke while we played the game.

Karma had just finished talking when she shifted—**eyes narrowing, posture stiffening just enough to clock something was up**. I followed her gaze.

Two men. Black suits. Moving toward us like they owned the floor.

"That must be them," she murmured, barely moving her lips.

They looked the part—calm, crisp, all business. One of them stepped forward first. "Hey there, I'm Agent Chen," he said, sliding into the booth like we were old friends. "This is Agent Jones. We're tasked with assisting you in your mission."

Smooth voice. Confident. The kind of guy who knows how to lie well. Definitely MIB.

I kept my expression neutral, but Karma? Her curiosity flared behind those sharp eyes. This was her first time working with MIB—**and I could tell she was low-key hyped about it.**

"We've been expecting you guys," she said, leaning forward just a bit. "Your organization's reputation precedes you."

They both nodded, easy and unbothered, as if this was just another Tuesday. Before the tension could thicken, a waitress rolled up beside us with a cart full of dim sum.

The scent hit instantly—hot steamed buns, crispy dumplings, five-spice wafting up with the steam. My stomach made its opinion known.

With a practiced flick, she popped open the lids on the metal trays. The aroma—**rich, savory, laced with garlic and sesame**— filled the booth like a spell. Karma lit up again. **Girl was in her element.** If we weren't mid-op, I think she might've ordered the entire cart.

"Evening," the waitress smiled. "Would you like some egg rolls? They're freshly made to order."

Our mouths were already watering.

"Yes, please," I said without hesitation. "And a round of Tsingtao beer, if you've got it."

Let the Earth games begin.

Karma answered before the words finished leaving the waitress's mouth. **"Yes—definitely, that one, that one, and—oh— definitely those."** Her stomach growled loud enough to make the waitress smile.

Karma didn't care. She was in full foodie mode, pointing at half the cart with that eager glint in her eye.

The waitress nodded and got to work, her hands a blur. **Golden-brown egg rolls hit the table with a crisp whis- per,**followed by steaming bamboo baskets filled with who-knew-what. Everything smelled ridiculous. Garlic, scallion, hoisin, spice—it all hung in the air like a warm blanket laced with hunger.

"Coming right up," she said, vanishing back into the kitchen like a ghost in flats.

We didn't wait. One bite into the egg rolls and the crunch hit like satisfaction incarnate. Hot, crispy shell. Savory filling. Real ingredients. Not synthetic. Not ration-packed. Actual Earth food.

But even with the flavor lighting up my brain, **the mission never left the front of my thoughts.** It pulsed beneath every bite.

Chen leaned forward, voice smooth but edged. "I have information that may interest you. There's a contact here in San Francisco—says he witnessed something unusual. Near a warehouse. Rumors say it houses a clandestine lab."

That snapped Karma out of her dumpling daze. She met my eyes—**silent communication charged with interest**.

I nodded once. "Go on."

Chen's gaze bounced between us, reading our reactions like a trained handler. "The contact was on a call near the wharf when he saw a sudden burst of light coming from one of the warehouses. Said it happened multiple times—same place, same intensity."

Bright light. Repeated events. That sounded familiar. Too familiar.

"He couldn't just ignore it," Chen went on. "Curiosity got the better of him. Said he circled the building—used his instincts, found a vantage point. Got a partial look inside."

His voice dipped lower, the words landing heavier now.

And just like that, the taste of the egg rolls vanished.

Something about the way Chen said it… **resourcefulness,

vantage point, contact—**it had that weight. That *this-shit's-real* kind of tone that made my spine straighten.

This wasn't just a lead.

It was the start of something bigger.

Karma and I leaned in as Chen started talking again, his voice a notch quieter, but heavy now. **Something had shifted.**

"He said he saw people inside—lab coats. Scientists, maybe. Then another bright light... and someone walked through it."

I froze. Just for a beat. **Walked through it.**

A portal.

Chen wasn't done. "He saw pods. Numbered. Stacked three high. Wrapped in shipping plastic. And small black boxes. Lots of them."

My stomach turned. Not from the food. From the picture forming in my head.

Pods and numbers?

That didn't sound like storage—it sounded like containment. Like someone was packaging something ... or someone.

The clink of glassware broke the silence as the waitress returned, balancing frosty bottles of Tsingtao in each hand. She smiled like nothing was wrong in the world. "Need anything else?" she asked brightly.

Chen answered in Chinese—**smooth, polite, a perfect local accent.** She nodded and disappeared, back into the haze of chatter and steam.

But the weight of what he'd said didn't leave with her.

Portal. Pods. Scientists. This wasn't just an abandoned lab. It was *active*. And whatever was going on in there? It was tied to the NexaHunt game. No question.

Karma glanced at me. We were synced on this—**we needed to meet that contact. Now.**

I turned to Chen. "We need to meet this guy. Do you have a lead? Time's running out—we can't afford to waste a single moment."

Chen met my eyes. His mask slipped for half a second—**just enough to show the tension underneath**. "Yeah. We've got his contact info. He's ready to cooperate... but we need to move fast."

He paused.

"We're not the only ones watching that warehouse."

Great. Of course we're not.

This mission just went from recon to sprint.

We leaned in close, heads almost touching over the plates. Voices low, serious. The kind of talk that could change everything.

Chen dropped the bomb like it was just another logistical hiccup. "We're short on manpower. You two will have to go in alone."

Perfect. Just what I wanted to hear. I gave a slow nod, jaw tight. No backup. Just us.

Around us, the restaurant kept buzzing.

Chopsticks clinked. Laughter bounced off lacquered wood.

Waitstaff slipped between tables with trays stacked high. None of it touched the conversation happening in this booth.

We kept eating like nothing was wrong. Pork buns, crispy dumplings, slippery noodles in soy broth. *Everything smelled incredible, tasted even better*—but none of it dulled the weight of the conversation. It just gave us cover.

The agents kept the flow casual—missions, tactics, a few vague war stories. Just enough to keep any eavesdroppers off the scent. But our focus? Laser sharp.

Karma and I traded a glance. We didn't wait.

"We've got something you need to hear," I said, dropping my voice lower. "There's been a pattern. Disappearances—players from the NexaHunt RPG. One of them was last seen right here. In this restaurant."

That got their attention. Even Jones sat up straighter.

"We were hoping you could help us track the thread," Karma said, voice steady but urgent. "Something isn't right. These disappearances aren't random."

Chen didn't respond right away. Just watched us like he was recalibrating the whole situation in real time.

I locked eyes with him. "The agency's been tracking them, yeah. But there's more to it."

I felt Karma's gaze on me before she spoke.

"Some of the players who come back... they're different. Changed. We don't know how or why—but the shift is real. Something about that warehouse feels connected. And we can't ignore it anymore."

That's what this is about. Not just the missing. The *damaged*. The ones who made it out, but didn't come back whole.

I leaned back slightly, scanning the room one more time. No obvious tails. No red flags.

But **everything in my gut told me we were on the edge of something massive.** The kind of truth people disappear for.

And we were walking straight into it.

Chen and Jones listened without interrupting, their faces etched with something I rarely saw on MIB types—**actual concern.** Eyes narrowed, brows knit. Not skepticism. **Interest. Alarm.**

Then—*cue the universe's perfect timing*—the waitress rolled up again, cart loaded to the edges. More dim sum. Four more beers. The scent of fried dough and steamed scallion hit us like a wave.

A wild contrast to the conversation we were knee-deep in.

you dig?

Anyway …

Karma didn't even hesitate. Reached straight for a bamboo steamer and cracked it open, her eyes lighting up like she hadn't just been talking about people vanishing through inter-dimensional portals.

"This is a puzzle we need to solve," she said between bites, her voice all steel now.

That was Karma. Sharp focus. Big appetite.

Mission never left her mind—even when her hands were full of dumplings.

We kept at it. Trading theories. Cross-referencing details. The clink of plates and low murmur of the restaurant faded into background texture, like white noise under our layered strategy session.

Something about that moment—*four people from completely*

different realities, huddled over food, sharing concern for a planet they didn't entirely belong to—it hit me.

This wasn't just an op anymore.

This was bigger. Intergalactic stakes. Human cost. A missing player here, a glitch in the system there—too many little pieces forming a pattern we couldn't ignore.

And somehow, over dumplings and cold beer, a kind of unity settled in. Purpose. Camaraderie. Call it what you want—we were locked in now.

When the meeting wrapped, there weren't any fancy good-byes. No dramatic walkouts. Just gratitude, real and quiet.

"Thank you," I said, meaning it.

Chen nodded. "Be careful."

They left with the same calm they arrived with, disappearing into the crowd like pros.

Karma and I sat there for a moment longer. Watching the door. Thinking about what came next.

Because whatever was waiting for us at that warehouse?

We were walking straight toward it.

"We'll be in touch," Chen said, tone steady like always.

Jones gave a quiet nod, echoing the promise without adding a word.

Karma and I watched as the two slipped out of the restaurant and into the blur of the crowd. **Suits swallowed by the city.** Ghosts in motion. Just like that, they were gone.

Karma didn't waste a second. She pulled the comm device from her pack and set it down between us with purpose. The screen lit up in soft blue, casting shadows across the plates and empty bottles. She opened the map app, fingers moving fast, deliberate.

"Let's see where this contact is," she muttered, already scanning.

I watched her work—**calm, focused, locked in**—and there was something sharp behind her eyes now. That spark. **She was ready.**

She tapped the screen, zoomed in, dropped a locator pin with precision. "Here," she said, lifting her gaze to mine. Her voice carried a charge. "This is where our path leads next."

I nodded once. No words needed. **We had a lead. We had a location. And we weren't stopping until we peeled the truth out of whatever waited at that warehouse.**

We grabbed our gear and slid out of the booth. The weight of the mission settled back into my spine like armor.

The moment we stepped outside, **the city hit us full-force**—horns blaring, voices clashing, lights blinking like a thousand restless eyes. Steam curled from sidewalk grates. Lanterns above swung in the wind. The scent of car exhaust mixed with fried garlic and incense.

San Francisco didn't sleep. And neither could we.

We moved through the crush of people, shoulders brushing, footsteps in sync. **Our destination glowed like a pulse point on the map—calling us forward.**

Time to hunt.

(((((O)))))

THE ALLEY WAS TUCKED JUST FAR ENOUGH off the main street to feel like a trap.

We arrived right on time—but still too late to be comfortable. The shadows here didn't just stretch—they leaned. Watched. Waited.

This was the meeting spot. Secluded. Exposed in all the wrong ways.

Karma and I didn't speak. Didn't need to. Every nerve in my body was on alert. My fingertips buzzed. My skin tracked shifts in pressure, like the atmosphere itself was holding its breath.

She stepped ahead, eyes already scanning the space. **Focused. Clinical. Ready.** Her attention locked onto a patch of cracked pavement just ahead.

"There," she said, voice low but sharp. She crouched, fingers hovering over faint burn marks etched into the ground. "Four distinct signatures. Portal use. Recent."

Right under our damn noses. Whoever we were meeting— they weren't amateurs.

Before I could say a word, movement stirred at the edge of the alley. A figure stepped out from the shadows, smooth and unhurried.

My eyes snapped to him. And yeah—he looked human. At first.

But the longer I stared, the more I saw what *wasn't right*. **The skin that reflected light just a little too perfectly. The eyes— too still. Too knowing.** Something behind the mask pulsed. Not human. Not fully.

His presence hit like a static charge. A hum beneath my skin.

We didn't move. Just watched. Measured. **Waiting to see which way this would break.**

He gave a single nod. That was all. But it told us what we needed—**this was the contact. The one Chen and Jones set us up with.**

"I know what you're after," he said. His voice had that layered quality—like it didn't come from his throat but from somewhere deeper. "And yes. The rumors about the warehouse are true."

He stepped closer. Just enough for us to feel the weight of what he wasn't saying.

"There's something shady going on in there," he warned. "But you have to be careful. That place is wired. Monitors in every corridor. AI-level surveillance. One wrong step…"

He didn't finish the sentence.

Didn't need to.

The weight in his voice said it all.

Whatever was happening inside that warehouse—it wasn't just illegal. It was dangerous. Controlled. Maybe even protected.

Karma and I locked eyes. We knew the drill.

Get in. Get answers. Don't get caught.

This just got real.

Our eyes met for a split second.

We didn't need to say it—we were both feeling it. The risk had just doubled. Whatever Mara was hiding, we were walking the blade's edge to find it.

The Contact led us to the side of the warehouse, slipping between the shadows like he belonged there. **We crept behind him, boots silent against the pavement, hearts drumming in sync.** He stopped near a boarded-up window, pried a narrow gap open with careful fingers.

We all leaned in.

Inside ... nothing.

An empty shell. Dust particles floated in angled shafts of light. The faint mechanical hum still buzzed somewhere in the background, but the main space? Cleaned out.

Too clean.

"There's nothing in there," Karma whispered, barely above the low drone of the warehouse's systems. Her voice was calm, but I could feel the tension coiled underneath. "We need evidence. Pictures. Anything."

The Contact blinked, visibly thrown. "This doesn't make sense," he muttered. "They were operating here two days ago. No signs of movement. How'd they clear it so fast?"

My jaw locked as I stared through the crack. **My thoughts went wild—what kind of tech moves a whole lab overnight? Did they teleport it? Mask it? Cloak it?** Or worse—was this place never real to begin with?

But Karma's voice cut through the spiral.

"We can't rush in blind," she said, eyes locked on the comm device as she worked a quick scan. "It's not worth getting caught. But we *can* gather intel discreetly."

Her calm steadied me. **She always had that gift—keeping me grounded when my instincts screamed to charge forward.**

"I don't get it," I muttered, still watching the empty space inside. "All those pods. Those black boxes. Gone without a trace? That takes serious resources."

She tapped a quick sequence on the device—pinging for background signals, hidden networks, maybe even residual portal data.

"We'll find the trace," she said. "They can move the operation, but they can't erase the footprint."

And that was the difference between panic and purpose. Between chasing ghosts... and tracking them.

Karma stared at the comm device, her expression tightening. "Man, they're clever," she muttered. "Our scanner's picking up heat signatures. People. Moving around in there."

I leaned over, eyes locking on the thermal readout.

The warehouse was anything but empty.

Faint pulses—four, maybe five—moving in slow, calculated paths. Like patrols. Or worse, scientists who *knew* how to hide.

I didn't hesitate. "Let's cloak and go inside."

She looked up. I saw the hesitation flicker behind her eyes, but she gave a short nod.

We tapped our belt toggles. A soft shimmer wrapped over us like liquid shadow. **Cloak engaged. Light bent around our forms, and the city lost sight of us.**

Blending into the warehouse perimeter, we crept closer. **Boots silent. Hearts loud.** Every door we checked—locked tight. Sealed like they were expecting us. No alarms, no signs of life, just cold metal and too many questions.

We couldn't brute-force it. One breach, and this whole op would blow wide open.

I turned to Karma, voice low but firm. "The portal devices," I said, tapping the buckle on my belt. "We use 'em. Port inside."

Clean. Fast. Controlled.

But Karma shook her head before I could finish. "Too risky," she whispered, scanning the warehouse again. "You know how unstable the portals are around high energy fields. This whole building's wired with tech. You open a portal in the wrong spot? We light up the whole grid like a firework."

She wasn't wrong. **Portals looked sleek in theory—silent, fast, surgical—but in practice? They could flash brighter than a solar flare and announce your location in five city blocks.**

Karma knelt, pulled up a schematic of the warehouse on her scanner. Blueprints flickered into view, lines pulsing faint blue.

"There," she said, pointing to a room on the lower floor. "Mechanical room. Far end of the building. Reinforced and mostly insulated. Big enough to port into."

I studied the map, checked the portal's calibration on my belt. Safe enough. Barely.

I nodded. "We go in quiet. One shot. We don't mess this up."

She looked at me, then tapped the coordinates into the portal device.

This was it. No turning back.

"On my count," I said.

Three. Two. One—

We vanished.

(((((O)))))

MY HEART WAS POUNDING as we slipped out of the portal—**straight into the mechanic's room** of the warehouse. Dim light. Concrete walls. The low hum of industrial generators masked the sound of our arrival.

Thank the stars. The cloaking held.

Karma and I moved in unison—**quiet, precise, fully alert.**

Every nerve was lit up, every muscle wired tight. We didn't speak. Didn't have to. **One wrong breath and we were done.**

But then… the comm pinged.

I glanced at the display—and froze.

NOLA?

Karma saw it too. Her brow furrowed hard, fingers flying across the screen, recalibrating.

"We were in San Francisco," she whispered. "What the hell—"

But there was no time to sort it out.

A faint glow slipped through the mechanic room doors—**soft, unnatural light, like something alive bleeding through the cracks.** We crept toward it, every step slower than the last.

We cracked the door just enough to slip through—right into the space we weren't supposed to see.

Pods. Dozens of them. Maybe more.

Rows upon rows, stacked three high, glowing dim blue. And inside?

Humans. Aliens. Clones. Suspended in hibernation—**each one locked in some kind of sleep paralysis**, faces masked by breathing apparatuses. Tubes ran into their mouths, wires clipped to their temples, eye ports, ear jacks. **Sensory override. Total lockdown.**

And somewhere close—**footsteps.**

I spun toward the sound.

A security guard. Walking straight toward the door we'd just slipped through, eyes locked on the lingering glow. **He hadn't seen us… but he felt something.**

He hesitated, hand drifting toward his sidearm.

Shit. One more second and we were toast.

We held still—**barely breathing**. The cloaking tech hummed against my skin, the microfield rippling with my heartbeat.

The guard stepped through the door—**and just missed us**. One step too late. One blink too slow.

We slipped past him like shadows.

Once inside the main chamber, I couldn't move. Couldn't breathe. Not properly.

This wasn't a warehouse. This was a goddamn farm.

Every pod was numbered. Cataloged. Controlled.

These weren't patients. They were products.

The sight hit like a gut punch. I couldn't move. Couldn't think.

Horror cracked through me, jagged and raw. These weren't just strangers. Weren't just test subjects. These were *people*. Living beings, locked in silence. Unseen. Unheard. Treated like things.

Like trophies.

Karma's breath hitched beside me. She raised the datapad, scanning one of the pods, fingers flying across the interface. The readout pinged. She went still.

"Trek…" she whispered, voice barely a thread. "This is sad. A NexaHunt player is hibernating."

My head snapped toward her. **What?**

I looked at the face behind the glass. Blank. Peaceful. Too peaceful. But familiar.

Recognition twisted into rage. My chest burned. My hands curled into fists.

That wasn't a patient. That was a *player*. Someone who signed up for a game—**not this.**

Movement pulled my eyes across the chamber.

Two figures. Barely visible through the haze and shifting lights. Talking in low voices between the rows of pods.

I narrowed my eyes.

Dr. Kael. Mara.

My blood went cold.

They were deep in conversation. I couldn't make out the words, but the intent hung thick in the air—**clandestine. Measured. Dangerous.**

And then Mara stopped.

Mid-sentence.

His head lifted.

Eyes scanning.

Shit.

Did he feel us? Sense the distortion in the air? The shift in energy that came with cloaking?

We were fifteen feet away. One misstep and this mission turned into a firefight.

Karma's voice hit my mind like a whisper behind my eyes. *Do you think he heard us?*

I didn't speak. Just nodded.

Then slowly, I raised my index finger.

Silence. No movement. No breath.

Mara's gaze swept the room—**calculating, searching, almost… tasting the space.** His eyes passed within inches of where we stood.

"What's wrong?" Kael asked, clearly sensing the shift in him.

But Mara didn't answer. Not right away.

And that silence? It was louder than any alarm.

"Wait," Mara whispered as he visually passed Kael with a hand up.

I felt the tension spike like a blade behind my ribs.

Mara was too close. Too aware.

I turned to Karma, gave the signal—**retreat. Now.** We'd seen enough. Logged the footage. Marked the faces. Every second we stayed was another second closer to getting caught.

She nodded, already tracking the path back through the pods.

No sound. No sudden movements. Just shadows slipping back through darkness.

We moved fast, ducking low, watching the patrol patterns on the scanner Karma held like a lifeline. The cloaking tech held, bending light, suppressing heat—barely.

Every breath I took felt tight in my chest.

One wrong step and we'd be those next pods.

We made it back to the mechanical room. No alarms. No sign of pursuit.

But my mind was racing. We had eyes on Kael. On Mara. We had proof. But we couldn't take them alone. Not yet.

And then there was the other thing. **The glitch.**

I checked my device again.

NOLA.

It still showed we were in New Orleans.

But we weren't.

I looked at Karma. She was staring at her readout too, brows pinched. "It says we're back in San Francisco," she whispered, voice tight. "It flipped again."

I didn't answer right away. My stomach twisted. **Something was wrong. Not just tech-wrong. Reality-wrong.**

We slipped outside, the alley swallowing us back up. No tail. No trace. Just the cold wind brushing past like a warning.

The informant drifted off into the night. I didn't care.

He was background now.

Karma turned to me. Eyes wide. Focused. Scared, but still grounded. I knew that look. I wore it too.

Something else is happening.

Something beneath the surface. Beneath Mara. Beneath Kael.

We didn't say it out loud—but we both *felt* it.

We couldn't go back inside tonight. Not while the predators were still home. But we couldn't walk away blind, either.

Karma reached into her gear and pulled out the drone—small, sleek, disguised to pass as debris.

I programmed it fast, locking in the **energy vibration signatures**—EVS—from everyone inside. Kael, Mara, the guards, the clones. Every living being had its own signature, and now?

We could track them. We could know who was who.

Karma placed the drone just inside the door, the soft click of the deployment confirming it was armed and live.

We backed away together, shadows vanishing down the alley.

We didn't speak.

But the next move?

It was already in motion.

"So much to do, so little time…" Karma muttered beside me, pacing in tight circles. "We can't leave this place, but we can't stay either. We need to contact Agents Chen and Jones. We've got to strategize our next move."

"Copy that," I said without thinking.

But even as I said it, **my focus slipped. Just for a second.** Something—off. Tugging at the edge of my mind like static.

Then I felt it.

"The girls," I said, the words barely formed before they left my mouth. "Something's wrong."

Karma turned, sharp. "What… what girls? Nenah and Kaya?"

I nodded, gaze already locked on the comm interface. "Their location beacons… they haven't moved in hours. Either they're stuck, or—" I cut myself off. **No. Don't say it.**

"They went off-grid?" Karma asked, voice dropping to a whisper.

I nodded again. "I used the TraceBeacons Dexx gave us. Both signals flatlined. No movement. No bounceback."

Karma's eyes darkened. She didn't say it, but I knew she was thinking the same thing I was.

Either they were captured… or worse.

Then—**a sharp, mechanical whir cut through the alley.**

Two drones burst from the warehouse rooftop, silent as death, their lights flicking in cold sequences. **Scanning. Systematic. Getting closer.**

Karma reacted first. "We've gotta move. Now."

No argument.

Adrenaline kicked back in, slicing through the dread like a blade. I scanned for an exit vector while she activated a short-term field disruption to scramble our heat sigs.

The moment our cloaking kicked in, we were shadows again—**but our thoughts weren't.** They were screaming.

Nenah. Kaya. Flatlined signals. The drones. The glitching coordinates.

Something big was moving under all of this. And we weren't ready. Not yet.

We disappeared into the night—no destination, just *away*. Safe enough to stop. To breathe. To think.

We needed downtime. Meditation. A systems reset. And a direct line to Nyx.

Because whatever was happening?

It was about to get worse.

CHAPTER 11
NOLA

SOMETHING HIT. **Hard.** Not physical—**internal.**

I staggered, the ground moved beneath my boots, tilting for a second.

Download.

A big one.

No warning, no buffer. Just raw data slamming into the mind implant like lightning in a brainstem.

I dropped to one knee, exhaling sharp.

Too much. Too fast.

Karma was at my side before I even called out—of course, she was. Her eyes locked with mine, already knowing. Our shared program synced up instantly, the neural link between us flaring to life.

We didn't speak. We didn't need to.

She knelt with me, forehead to forehead.

The moment locked in. One heartbeat, two. Then the data unfolded like a waking dream—**and we were both inside it.**

Everything. Real time. She saw what I saw. *No filter, no delay.*

Images. Coordinates. Symbolic overlays.

The city pulsing like a living grid beneath us.

Three shapes. **Circle. Triangle. Square.**

But not just geometry—**markers. Anchors.**

And something deeper. A feeling buried beneath the code. Urgency. Destiny. *This was the next phase.*

We pulled back from the shared stream, breathless. That short, instinctive hug grounded us like gravity. **The world rushed back in—heat, jazz, static.** Reality roaring behind our eyes.

I stood, nodding once to Karma. She nodded back.

It had begun.

(((((O)))))

THE DATA STREAM HIT HARD—FULL immersion spike.

I blinked once. The simulation took over.

Dexx's interface was already running full tilt, mapping the sensory field from Kaya's pack and syncing it with Karma's uplink.

> *If you're wondering whats going on here. Imagine Karma and I watching in real-time Kaya and Nenah's experiences VIA the implant—the mind link device.*

Holographic overlays built the world around us piece by piece —projected jazz, heat shimmer, cityscape curves.

New Orleans wrapped around us in ghostlight.

We weren't there. Not physically. But our minds? **Locked in.**

Karma leaned forward beside me on the bench, eyes tracking every micro-movement. "Stabilization looks good. Kaya's biometrics are spiking, but Nenah's keeping her grounded."

"I see it," I said. "She's leading."

Kaya nearly stepped off the rooftop, and Nenah caught her.

"Careful. We can't afford any mistakes."

Her voice echoed in our ears, reconstructed through the neural mic embedded in the pack's strap. Dexx's system caught the tones, filtered out the wind.

Karma smiled faintly. "Nenah's control is next-level."

We watched as Kaya blinked and finally tuned into the world around her—**color bloom activating,** jazz vibrations pulled through sub-harmonic threads in the soundfeed.

"Rendering Creole spice," I muttered, tapping the air to slow the scent overlay. "Damn. Dexx outdid himself."

"Has the first item shown up?" Kaya asked.

I paused the feed for a second and zoomed in.

Karma was already pulling up the heatmap—Jackson Square lit up like a pressure point.

Tarot booths. Street performers. Locals mixed with tourists.

It was alive. But it wasn't just alive—it was charged.

Nenah's gaze swept the square. We watched through her eyes.

They moved fast—down the stairs, into the crowd.

"I'm ready to kick some butt," Kaya said.

Adrenaline. Confirmed.

Then Kaya shifted.

Her attention locked in on a tarot booth at the edge of the square. Our HUD tagged the reader in real time—**Estrella**—name floating in old script above her head. The algorithm flagged her aura signature: *off the charts.*

"Look at this," Karma said, magnifying the aura's pulse.

"She's not local," I said, voice low. "She's planted."

Kaya and Nenah moved closer.

Incense hit first. The chemical composition pinged instantly—frankincense, myrrh, dragon's blood. **Thick stuff. Sacred stuff.**

Estrella's face appeared in high-res on our upper pane. Black mirror eyes. Smile like déjà vu.

"She flipped the cards like she's done this in every timeline," Karma said.

We both leaned in as her voice came through the feed, soft, calibrated, laced with intention.

"You seek solace and clarity in this vast universe. You will find it when three symbols align at your feet: a circle, a triangle, and a square."

Karma whispered, "That's the activation code."

Every part of me locked up.

I watched Nenah and Kaya exchange looks. Nenah's skin prickled—I felt it echo through the relay.

"Three symbols," Nenah repeated, running calculations behind her eyes. "She knows something, Kaya. **This isn't just a random fortune."**

Kaya nodded, her expression sharpening. "Let's keep moving. We'll figure it out as we go."

We watched them stand. Step back. Leave Estrella behind.

But the data didn't fade.

Karma exhaled, voice quiet: "She dropped a ripple."

I nodded. "This timeline just forked."

We stayed in the holographic haze as Kaya and Nenah moved on—**but the weight of Estrella's words stayed anchored in the stream.**

The heat didn't touch us. Not directly. But the moment Kaya and Nenah stepped into the antique shop, the data stream shifted.

Dense. Oppressive.

The humidity registered at 97% through Kaya's back-strap sensor. Our system caught the spike.

"Feels like New Orleans is trying to swallow them whole," I muttered, leaning forward as the full sensory overlay wrapped around the observation rig.

Karma didn't blink. "The environment's reactive. Dexx's build is holding—barely."

The hologrid painted the inside of the shop around us— cracked wood, faded wallpaper, glass cases cluttered with relics. The scent overlay kicked in: **old wood, mildew, the iron-tang of aged metal.**

My neural feed translated the air like a forgotten attic.

Kaya moved toward a shelf, slow, drawn.

"There," I said.

She reached out. Finger to silver. The visual spike hit our monitors before she even flinched.

The pocket watch.

Karma's brow lifted slightly. "There it is."

I magnified the object, paused the loop on Nenah stepping into frame beside her.

"That's James Walker's pocket watch," she said, voice clear through the synched audio relay.

"Confirmed," I muttered. "We lost that artifact six cycles ago. Dexx thought it was off-grid."

"Well," Karma said, shifting her view, "looks like it just respawned."

Kaya turned the watch over. **Curious. Confident. No fear.** The curse? She didn't buy it. I watched her pulse spike anyway—just slightly.

The shopkeeper entered frame like a ghost. Creepy smile, too many secrets in his teeth. Kaya worked him for info. He spun the tale. My gut twisted.

"Standard cursed object story," I said. "But it's too clean. This is placed."

Karma nodded. "Agreed. The energy signature around that watch hasn't degraded. Someone preserved it. For this."

Nenah looked at Kaya.

"We'll take it," Kaya said.

Transaction complete. The artifact was theirs.

But the second they stepped outside?

Everything changed.

The weight of that watch did something. Kaya's readings jittered. Nenah's scan went tight—hyperaware.

"I'm getting hungry," Kaya said aloud. But the tone beneath?

She was clocking the threat.

"Movement," Karma said, pointing to a red blip flaring up on the satellite tracker. "They're being followed."

I traced the location overlay as they headed down Royal, then Toulouse. Café Du Monde marked on their map—crowds, noise, safe zone.

"They're going to try and disappear," I said. "Smart."

Then came the shift—footsteps, too synchronized. **Echoing through the audio feed like a drumbeat under the jazz.**

"Keep moving," Nenah said. Her voice low. Leveled.

The tension cracked. They broke formation. Quick turns. Alley run.

"Kaya's panic response is flaring," Karma said. "But she's channeling it."

We watched the whole thing unfold like a live-action sim— bouncing off dumpsters, cutting through dead-end heat. Kaya looked back. Face said it all.

"There!" she shouted.

A fire escape.

Two henchmen on the radar. **Confirmed ID—Mara's people.**

"Nenah moved first," I said. "Classic ISAD instincts, and she doesn't even know."

They climbed fast. We tracked vitals. Kaya missed a step, caught herself. Adrenaline dumped into her bloodstream like an open floodgate.

They hit the roof.

"Keep moving!" Nenah snapped. Even through the digital relay, her voice cut through the chaos.

They ran. Hologrid built the rooftop-scape in front of us like a dream stitched from concrete and sweat. Then—

Gap. Wide. Too wide.

"Jump!"

They flew.

Hard landings. Scans showed minor impact bruises, elevated vitals—but no hesitation.

"They're in it now," Karma said softly, watching the trail of their heat signatures fade behind them.

I didn't say anything right away. **Just watched them run.**

Watched them disappear over the next rooftop.

Watched the pocket watch in Kaya's bag glow just a little too bright.

"Whatever this game is," I finally said, "it's evolving."

Karma tapped something on the control surface, locking in a timestamp. "And it's watching them right back."

Kaya stumbled, but she regained her footing; Nenah grabbed her arm and steadied her.

"Come on, we can't stop now!" Nenah urged, pulling Kaya to her feet.

We tracked them as they hit the rooftop. The landing was hard—Nenah took the brunt, Kaya stumbled, but they were up fast. Moving. Survivors.

Karma and I watched in silence as the chase data faded from the stream. **Pulse rates dropped.** Adrenaline bleeding out. Sound filters caught the slowdown—footsteps fading, the echo of danger shifting into background noise.

Then—**Café Du Monde.**

The location scan was almost too normal: fried dough, chicory coffee, sticky air. But the neural overlay never lies. Kaya sat across from Nenah, back straight, eyes scanning like she still expected a sniper from the sugar line.

"Is it part of the illusion?" Kaya asked.

Karma glanced at me, reading the tension. "She's onto it."

Nenah didn't answer right away. The food came through the stream in scent bursts—sweet, fried, sharp with powdered sugar. The emotional resonance in Kaya's voice cut deeper than the flavor.

"Feels staged," she said. **"Like the game's guiding us... but not how we think."**

"She's not wrong," I muttered.

Karma tapped into the artifact cache interface. "Watch this."

Nenah reached into her bag. Pulled the pocket watch out again.

Click.

We both leaned in as she opened the back. Tiny compartment. Hidden until now.

Parchment.

Dexx's system couldn't scan it from here—too small, too encrypted. But **the microcam feed let us read the writing once it unrolled.**

I figured it out. Everything is energy. Let's meet later.

Programmer.

My jaw tightened. "Programmer again."

"They're lacing this in now," Karma said. "Breadcrumbs inside relics. Like someone's hacking the game from within."

Before we could go deeper, **studio notification buzzed in the audio feed**. Kaya flinched like she'd expected it. Nenah just watched the clue appear on their wrist console.

Where can you get an Enola Gay trinket?

Kaya's eyes lit up.

"WWI Museum. Let's go."

I sat back. "Wrong."

Karma smirked. "Close enough. WWII museums already flagged in their route system."

Nenah adjusted the datapad—got the right lock.

"We need to beat them to it."

They moved fast—**shadows along Decatur**, Dexx's tech painting them over the real map like ghosts in motion.

Karma synced the sat-view. "You see that?"

"Yeah," I said. "Someone else is watching them, too."

Surveillance lines blinked in the background. Cameras not connected to NexaHunt. Too smooth. Too buried.

Kaya glanced over her shoulder—pure instinct. Not paranoia.

"She felt it," Karma whispered.

"They're not just playing," I said. "They're being played."

And the game? **Still watching.**

CHAPTER 12
UPGRADE

THE PORTAL FLARE bloomed on the feed like lightning through static. Neural HUD flickered once, stabilized. Visual sync locked.

Restroom. Earthside. Small space. Two targets. Not alone.

I leaned forward, elbows resting on my thighs, watching the hologrid reconstruct the scene in real time. Kaya and Nenah had just exited the jump gate—and materialized right into a stall-level situation.

"Seriously, Dexx? Couldn't code them into a back alley like normal people?"

Karma didn't flinch. "Maybe someone rerouted the exit point."

"Yeah. Or the game's evolving."

On the screen: two Earthlings. One blonde—mid-sip of lipstick. The other, short black hair, perched on the toilet, eyes glued to her phone.

Social media dopamine coma.

Classic.

Then she looked up.

Shock. Smile. Giddy curiosity.

"Damn, where did you blue-skinned ninja chicas come from?"

I blinked.

Karma zoomed in, recalibrating the emotion pulse signature. "They saw them. Full form."

"They shouldn't be able to."

Blonde's eyes dropped to Kaya's wrist. No fear. Just awe. Recognition? Attraction?

Her dropped lipstick rolled across the tile.

"Y'all ain't seen nothing,"

Wooh… Did you get that? Kaya responded telepathically.

Karma laughed through her nose. "That girl's bold."

But what came next hit harder.

Nenah scanned the women.

"Are you seeing what I'm seeing?

They have OUR DNA!"

I froze.

"They're tagged," I said.

"That's ISAD-buried gene sequencing. Or someone's copying us."

Karma checked the cross-reference. "I'm not getting a match in our records… yet."

"How is that possible?" Kaya whispered.

On the wall behind them: a faded poster. **"Cured on Columbia."**

"What the hell is this place?"

"Off-map convergence point," Karma replied. "Interdimensional bleed. Like a pocket hub."

We watched Kaya and Nenah steady themselves, then exit the restroom.

(((((O)))))

VISUAL SYNC TRANSITION:

Front café camera.

Ambient feed captured through satellite microdrone.

They stepped into a rustic café—**Cured**, apparently.

The air glowed warm. Conversation hum. Glasses clinking. Music threading through a soft stereo.

Their posture shifted—Kaya especially. **Shoulders loose. Smile real.**

"They feel safe here," I murmured.

The Earthling girls came out of the restroom, *giggling* as if they'd just spotted celebrities in cosplay.

One **poured herself a whiskey**.

The other cleaned her glasses like she'd seen a damn ghost.

"Could we be hallucinating?" the blonde asked.

I marked their body language. **Not hallucinating—processing.**

"They *did* see them," Karma said.

"They shouldn't be able to," I repeated. "Unless—they're not fully Earthling," Karma finished.

The data streams over the women were glitchy.

Partial IDs. Fragmented bio-sig. Like the system didn't know what to classify them as.

"Let's grab a bite," Kaya said.

"No, we don't have time for that."

The shift was fast. Mission mode. *Kaya's instincts kicked back* in.

"Let's get out of here."

They exited quick, **disappearing** into the street crowd.

Karma tapped her console. "Street view's open. Carnival atmosphere. Halloween week."

"Good cover," I said. "They'll blend."

On the corner, someone in a jack-o'-lantern mask tossed confetti into the air. Nenah and Kaya didn't flinch. They merged with the flow like they'd done it a hundred times.

But I could feel it in my chest—**something's off.**

The scene was soft. Light. But the game?

It was just about to bite.

(((((O)))))

STREET. **Motorcycle . Upgrade Notification**

The feed kept pulsing.

Kaya and Nenah emerged from the café into a street that looked like a cyberdream and a costume party collided.

Cars lined up like chrome beetles. Motorcycles glinting under streetlights.

Revelers moved in packs—masks, glitter, fog machines, jazz remixes in the air.

Halloween week in New Orleans.

They slipped into the current like ghosts. **Two more faces.** No one questioned them.

But I was watching.

"You feel that?" I asked quietly.

Karma leaned closer, tapping her tablet like she could physically sift through the vibes.

"Yeah. There's something in the flow. Like a static pocket following them."

The crowd's energy wasn't just festive—it was too perfect. Like someone wanted them relaxed. **Disarmed**.

Then Nenah stopped. She saw it before I did—a motorcycle on display. Black and chrome, matte finish, soft blue glow under the body. Old Earth aesthetic, but souped up with tech enhancements. **Energy-based drive shaft.** Probably custom.

She froze.

"Look at her vitals," Karma said. "She's hypnotized."

"She's back in her element," I whispered. "That's good. Could ground her."

Then—

Buzz. Overlay distortion.

My HUD shimmered.

On Kaya's device: an incoming notification.

UPGRADE AVAILABLE: ENHANCE GAMEPLAY. FIX MINOR GLITCHES. RECOMMENDED.

"Nope," I said immediately.

Karma was already pulling up backend diagnostics. **"Not ours. Not Dexx's code. This is native to the NexaHunt OS."**

I opened a channel. "Dexx, you seeing this?"

His voice crackled through. Crisp, composed. "Yeah. I caught it about six seconds before it hit their feeds. That's not ISAD-sanctioned. That's... something embedded in the player-side framework."

"Could it compromise their hardware?"

"It's not malware," he said. "But I wouldn't call it clean either. It's... persuasive. It wants root access."

I clenched my jaw. "So it's a permission trap."

"Looks that way. Want me to block it from our end?"

"No. Let it ride. I need to see what they choose."

Kaya stared at the comm device in her hand. Her hesitation was **beautiful and terrifying.**

"Trust... I don't trust anyone that's not you," she told Nenah.

"Smart girl," Karma muttered.

But then—

Kaya tapped ACCEPT.

The download initiated.

The progress bar crawled. **Slow. Deliberate.** Almost as if it wanted them to think about it.

I watched the device hum softly, overlay beginning to flicker with a pixel-tear. Nenah leaned over, watching it load. Her expression: uncertain. Cautious. Too late.

"They've taken the bait," I said under my breath.

Then **Karma pointed at a spike on her feed.**

"Wait. Look at Nenah's side channel. Her comms didn't activate the same way. She's watching Kaya's download, but not mirroring it."

"So she's stalling."

"Or she knows something she's not saying."

The data field around them shimmered. Kaya's emotional frequency dropped three points. **Subtle fear. Buried well.** But not enough to fool me.

Dexx pinged in again. "If she completes this update, you're going to lose some visibility. The signal obfuscation is kicking in."

"How much?"

"Fifteen to twenty percent blind spot."

"Can you trace who coded it?"

Pause. Dexx sighed. "No origin stamp. No trace signature. Whoever did this is good. Too good."

That hit different.

Karma looked up at me. "We need to make a call. Intervene or stay in observation mode."

I didn't answer right away.

Because in that moment, as the crowd danced around them, as neon bounced off rain-wet asphalt, as Kaya stared at her glitching interface like it might bite her...

I felt it.

That old instinct. The one I trained to ignore. The one that never lies.

We're not the only ones watching them anymore.

(((((O)))))

POST-UPGRADE GLITCH. **Cassette Hunt. Record Store**

Kaya's download completed.

That was the moment everything changed.

Her feed jittered. Display stuttered—visual data warped like bad analog. Images broke apart into flickering fragments. Text overlays twisted, glitching in and out like someone was tuning reality on the wrong frequency.

"Faaahhhh... something's wrong..." Kaya's voice cracked through the implant feed. "The upgrade must've caused this."

Bingo.

I leaned forward, eyes locked on the readouts. Her device wasn't just bugged—it was compromised.

Karma pinched the live telemetry feed. "She's getting null loops. **Feedback echo.** Someone's hijacked her signal integrity."

Nenah's screen lit up in parallel—same glitch. "Damn it," she hissed. "We need a fix."

But they didn't have time. The next scavenger clue popped right through the digital noise, like it had been waiting for chaos to hit.

"Find a cassette of a musical group named Duran Duran."

I blinked.

Karma just said it: "Too convenient."

They'd barely recovered from the glitch and already they were moving. Kaya tried to recalibrate, her touchpad flickering between static and a mangled version of the game's interface.

"Without the map, we're lost," she told Nenah. "We need to log the item ASAP. **Reset these devices.**"

They made a call—and pivoted. Fast. Their momentum was admirable, even if the path was baited.

We watched as they followed the beat down a narrow strip of street—music blasting, people dancing, a block party in full riot-mode joy. Their body language said calm. Their heart rate said otherwise.

Then I saw it.

Convergence point.

"Pause feed," I said. Karma froze it mid-frame.

Overlay lit up in neon script:

Cured

Black Flower Apparel & Records

"You see it?" I asked.

Karma nodded slowly. "Convergence event. I've only seen one of these. Covington."

"Multidimensional rest stop. Not officially part of the game."

"They won't even know what they walked into."

"Or who else is watching?"

(((((O)))))

VISUAL RESUMED.

A bell above the record shop door jingled.

Inside: a man with dreadlocks. Smile bright. Hands steady.

The moment Nenah and Kaya stepped inside, the energy shifted. Dexx's sensor grid picked it up immediately—low hum across the EM spectrum. An old signal. Analog and ancient.

"Astronaut," Karma whispered.

"What?"

"The song. It's Duran Duran. Track from the reunion album. The system synced the song to the clue."

"So they're being led."

Inside, Kaya split off. Her attention locked on a man across the room.

Wild white hair. Thick glasses. Lime green streak curling above his eyebrow. Every ethnicity coded into his face.

Kaya moved toward him like her instincts weren't her own.

"Who the hell is that?" I murmured.

Karma tapped the DNA trace.

My **stomach dropped.**

"He's tagged," she whispered. "Same as the girls from the café bathroom. And... same as Kaya."

"Another hybrid."

"And he knows," she added. "He saw them the moment they walked in."

Nenah was already at the cassette wall. The dreadlocked shop owner guided her—cool, chill, as if this was all part of some ritual. He pointed toward the ceiling speakers. "Just listen," he said.

The beat pulsed. Kaya and Nenah found the Duran Duran section.

That's when the tech started frying.

Kaya stared at her device, frustration boiling behind her eyes. Garbled text. Jittering UI. **Flickers of ghost-code.**

"Is yours malfunctioning too?" Nenah asked.

Her screen was worse. Pixel death, scattered sigils, unreadable glyphs.

"Dexx, what are we seeing?" I asked, already queuing his uplink.

"Feedback loop," he answered. "The upgrade didn't just patch —it rewrote core display logic. They're not just blind. They're vulnerable."

"They need to log the item," Karma said. "But the system's corrupted."

"They're losing map access. Marker placement's gone."

"Without the map, we're lost," Kaya said again. "We have to reset. Fast."

They stepped out onto a bench just outside the shop.

Kaya's frustration spiked. She gripped the comm and hissed:

"HA! Trust Mara ... what a mistake!"

Karma exhaled sharply. "She said his name."

"Then it's confirmed," I said. "Mara coded the upgrade."

"And now we know."

But their voices dropped as the crowd volume rose again. A parade rolled by. Fire breathers. Dancers. Masked jesters. Kaya's rage bled into the cityscape, but Nenah pulled her back.

They walked.

Then something fluttered.

A crumpled brochure.

Kaya paused—scanned it.

I zoomed in with a two-finger flick. Karma amplified the image. There, on the front: **a circle. A triangle. A square.**

"Find Solace at the New Orleans Zen Temple."

"Ohhhh damn," Karma whispered.

"Game just got spiritual," I muttered.

And just like that—they were moving again. No longer chasing clues.

Now they were chasing something that felt like truth.

(((((O)))))

ZEN TEMPLE. **Haruto. Inner Shift**

The moment Kaya picked up that brochure, everything about the feed changed.

Frequency drop.

It wasn't just the image of the Zen Temple or the symbols on the paper. It was the way the system reacted to them.

Noise levels dropped. Light saturation dipped. **Emotional signatures narrowed like pupils adjusting to sacred space.**

Karma caught it too. "We're losing sensor fidelity."

"No," I said. "The feed's adapting."

We watched Kaya show the flyer to Nenah—three symbols glowing at the top.

Circle. Triangle. Square.

The same ones Estrella pulled in her tarot spread.

"Let's recharge there," Kaya said.

They turned around. Moved with purpose.

I pulled the camera feed wide, saw them head back toward Cured, entered the restroom again.

Portal activated.

Destination: New Orleans, alleyside. Just outside the Temple's perimeter.

> Environmental Sync: NOLA → Zen Temple Perimeter
>
> Status: Partially Interference-Shielded
>
> Analysis: Dimensional energy signature detected
>
> Access: Passive observation only

They exited the portal and immediately the vibe snapped.

Kaya's device glitched, but Nenah's synced clean. Karma noted it.

"She's stable. Kaya's still pulsing off the upgrade."

"System conflict," I said. "She's fighting the interface."

They walked until they spotted a rickshaw. Unironic. Unapologetic.

I smiled. "Of course."

As they rode, Kaya and Nenah finally slowed down. Not just their movement—their energy. Dexx's biometric feed showed it: adrenaline dropped, cortisol dipped. **Theta waves rising.**

"They're shifting," Karma said. "Tuning down."

Then—arrival.

Zen Temple. High-frequency zone. The noise of the city filtered out like someone hit mute.

"What is this place?" I whispered.

Karma was already **tracing architecture**. "Interdimensional frequency field. Stone matched to vibrational ley lines. Monks here don't meditate. They resonate."

The gates opened.

Nenah and Kaya stepped through the sanmon entrance.

(((((O)))))

INSIDE: **silence. Flowing water. Rustling leaves.** Temple walls radiated earth-toned energy. Dexx's implants picked up traces of Nag Champa, cherry blossom pollen, oxygen-rich air.

They paused.

"Wow, did you feel that?" Kaya asked.

Nenah didn't even answer. Her breathing slowed. Her stance changed.

I felt something too—a compression in my chest.

Not anxiety. Not interference.

Stillness.

And then he entered the frame.

Haruto.

The monk.

The Roshi.

The variable we didn't see coming.

His presence hit hard. Visual overlay glitched for half a second —not because of signal loss, but because the system couldn't lock onto his frequency.

He looked into their eyes and said,

"Welcome."

Then I heard it.

Karma straightened. "Did you feel that?"

I nodded. "He just scanned them. Not tech. Energy."

We watched them follow Haruto into the temple. Outdoor gardens. Cherry blossoms. Koi pond. Candles and wind and time moving like a breath.

They sat. Finally. No comms. No triggers. No clues to decode.

And Kaya broke the silence.

"Haruto, we need to tell you something... We're from a parallel universe. We came through an interdimensional portal."

Haruto didn't even blink.

"Ah. I presumed as much."

Nenah added—"We're playing a scavenger hunt game," like that made it lighter.

But the way he responded?

"You're not the first to visit us from another world. Some don't even know they're from another world."

That line hit like a key turned inside a locked door.

"Pause," I whispered.

Karma froze the feed.

I stared at Haruto's image on the screen. **That smile. Those eyes.**

"He's more than a monk."

"He's not even surprised," Karma said. "He's seen us before."

Us. Not them.

I didn't answer.

We resumed the feed.

(((((O)))))

HARUTO LED them deeper into the temple. They walked through carved halls. Pillars etched with timelines. Statues older than Earth's known history.

Then—the courtyard.

"Those are our evolved monks," Haruto said. "They phase in and out of matter. Train beyond physics."

We watched them shift. Slip between dimensions like it was muscle memory.

"They vibrate at higher frequencies. Thoughts become force."

Nenah and Kaya stood speechless.

Kaya—who usually had a quip for everything—just watched.

And something changed in her. I saw it in the feed.

The armor dropped. The fire within didn't flare—it deepened.

Purpose. Stillness. Power.

When Kaya whispered:

"Thank you for reminding us what matters,"

… I felt that in my spine.

Haruto smiled.

"The present moment is a series of milliseconds of consciousness."

He bowed.

Dexx pinged me just then. "You still watching this?"

"Every frame," I said.

"Feed's clean. But you're off the grid."

"Good," I said. "Let's keep it that way."

Because for once…

Watching felt like witnessing.

Karma an I had nothing to say.

Only to feel.

CHAPTER 13
RUN

THE TEMPLE BELL faded into silence. And for a while… the stillness stayed.

I tracked Kaya's and Nenah's movements as they walked the city streets. **Their vitals had never looked this stable—resting heart rates, breath synced, theta levels still humming from that last Zazen round.**

"Grounded," Karma murmured behind me, reading the same scans I was. "We should've gone with them."

"We couldn't," I said. "We were never meant to reach them yet."

She exhaled. "Feels like the game's changing."

It was.

They walked with purpose, but it wasn't adrenaline. It was intention. Until Kaya's comm blinked—a message. From me.

I saw her eyes light up before the feed caught the actual holochat. Her joy wasn't loud, but it pulsed through the tracker in my chest. **Like a note struck on the edge of memory.**

"Trek. We miss you guys. What part of the city did you arrive in?"

That voice. Familiar in ways I couldn't explain.

"We were misdirected," I told her. "San Francisco."

She winced. "Whoa. That's a mess."

She didn't ask for blame. Just wanted to know how to fix it. That was her style—fix what's broken, even if she didn't break it.

"We disconnected from the RPG," she continued. "We stayed the night at a temple… We were pursued."

That word. **Pursued.**

"Not by other players," Nenah said. "By something pretending to be Earthling. But it wasn't."

"Its energy was all wrong," Kaya added. "Alien. And angry."

The feed tightened. Their posture had changed. Not in fear—but in readiness.

"We'll try to reach you soon," I told them. "Be safe."

"We will."

The moment she cut the feed, I felt it. A drop in my chest. **Like I'd just let my sister walk into a war zone.**

Karma caught it. "You okay?"

I nodded. "I just…"

I paused.

She feels like someone I lost.

And then… a voice chimed in from my comm.

"Agent 417."

Director NYX.

Her voice was silk wrapped around steel.

"Report."

"Still tracking the lead team," I said, standing up. "They're active. Minimal contact. System updates have caused instability."

"We've noticed," she said. "The upgrade corrupted more than we thought."

"Any movement on the second team?" I asked.

"No trace," she replied. "But we've intercepted fragments of **unauthorized portal traffic.** Someone's jumping without clearance. Possibly linked."

There was silence between us. One beat. Two.

"Find them. All of them."

Then her voice softened.

"You good at watching Trek. But this may require more."

She cut the channel.

I stared at the screen.

Kaya and Nenah. Walking. Smiling. Eating pizza handed over by some stranger with tattoos. Kaya flirting. Nenah observing.

Then Nenah's vitals changed.

Fear spike. Slight. Controlled.

"We're being followed."

I zoomed in.

Two shadows. One pulse-staggered. The other—cloaked. Not human.

They bolted.

Into an alley. Rooftop run. Footsteps pounding. Fear blooming in real time. Kaya's heart rate climbing, steady but wild.

Then Kaya stopped. Paused.

Rooftop edge.

"Trust me," Nenah said.

They jumped.

And that's when it hit me.

...for a second, I felt the echo of him.

The breath against my shoulder.

The pause before the leap.

The last time I looked back.

That was the mission I didn't come back from whole.

(((((O)))))

FLASHBACK

The air had smelled like burnt ozone.

The last safe zone was twenty meters behind us.

And he'd still been smiling.

I told him we'd make it.

He said, *"You first."*

I never saw him again.

(((((O)))))

THE SOUND of Kaya landing snapped me back.

They hit the solar-paneled roof and crawled up—panting, trembling, alive.

For now.

Karma's voice cut in. "I'm losing feed clarity."

"Boost the relay," I said. "We're not dropping them again."

Then the visual popped.

An old woman. Grocery bag. Big sunglasses.

"Are you okay, my little darlings?" she asked.

Kaya and Nenah hesitated. She radiated warmth. She was too perfect. But not a threat. They followed her.

Inside: Creole cottage. 1940s decor.

Old music. Stories of New Mexico. Atomic testing. Family ties.

She said her mother worked on the Manhattan Project.

She said the man in the photo might be her father.

Karma and I both froze.

"That's Mara's dad," she whispered.

There it was. The fracture point. **The past bleeding into the present.**

They stayed for a while. Ate. Laughed. Played cards.

It felt like safety.

But safety was never real in this game.

(((((O)))))

ALERT.

Nenah's tracker spiked. Sickening pressure.

"Karma."

"I see it—movement. Black van. No ID markers."

My stomach dropped.

"Get me audio—NOW."

But it was too late.

Pop. Pop.

Two shots.

Both trackers went red.

Kaya. Nenah. Down.

I stood up fast. The chair behind me clattered to the floor.

"Lock onto the shooter. Trace the van. Override their systems. I want visuals, weapon scans, trace routes—"

My pulse thundered.

Because I'd stayed in the shadows too long.

And now the light was calling.

This is no longer a game.

This is a mission.

I pulled up my holomap.

Agent 417: Activated.

CHAPTER 14
ANDROID ENCOUNTER

THE SILENCE WASN'T JUST quiet—it was wrong.

"Kaya, respond."

Pause. Static.

"Nenah, if you hear this—ping us back. Anything."

Still nothing.

I tried again. Changed frequencies. Boosted signal. Nothing but digital breath.

Karma stood across from me, arms crossed, fingers drumming against her datapad. **Not tapping. Drumming.** That only happened when she was masking dread.

"They should've answered by now," she said.

"They're alive," I replied. But even I could hear the friction in my voice.

For now.

I scanned the neural feeds again—subtle, fading blips of electromagnetic scatter. **Not total silence**, but close. Like listening for a heartbeat through water.

You don't need a pulse monitor to know someone's in trouble.

Kaya's last location pinged faintly before it flickered out completely. Her biofeedback was still there—but it had gone cold, muted, like it was passing through layers of interference.

Something was jamming them. Or worse.

"417." Director Nyx's voice sliced through the comms like a blade through silk.

"We've lost signal from five ISAD agents across three sectors. Portal tampering confirmed. Unregistered jumps. This isn't isolated."

Her voice dropped, just a decibel. Enough to press into your spine.

"Whatever Mara's building—it's moving faster than we estimated. Find them."

The line cut out. **No goodbye.** Just mission parameters.

I looked at Karma. "We're going."

She didn't argue. Just nodded and pulled the mobile portal ring from her belt. I locked in coordinates to New Orleans.

We stepped through.

(((((O)))))

FRENCH QUARTER. **Late.**

We landed in a piss-smelling alley two blocks from Bourbon. A drunk sat in the corner with a bottle labeled Grey Funeral.

He looked up at us—two armed agents materializing from an interdimensional shimmer—and just grinned.

"Greg," he slurred. "Jim."

Karma stepped over him. I followed. "Better than being sober," I muttered.

We cut through the night—neon lights bleeding against wet pavement—until we reached The Pit Stop burger joint. Inside, wedged in the corner, was Agent Krix. Clean-cut, tactical mind, **eyes like live wire.**

He didn't greet us. Just slid a drive across the table.

"Surveillance footage. Girls were picked up. Shot in the back. Unmarked black van. No plates. Military movement."

I watched the feed. Kaya went down first—fast. Nenah second. **The hit was clean. Professional.**

Karma closed her eyes. "This wasn't random."

"No," I said. "This was Mara."

Krix glanced toward the door, lowered his voice. "Last known drop was at a house nearby. Belongs to an older Earth woman. We think she might've given them shelter."

"You're coming?" I asked.

He shook his head. "My clearance got blocked by someone above me. This is all you."

Karma and I left the joint without another word.

(((((O)))))

MS. ANN'S HOUSE. **Creole-style. Frozen in time.**

The door creaked open. She didn't even flinch.

"Can I help you?" she asked.

I stepped forward. "Did two girls come here? Nenah and Kaya?"

Her brows furrowed. "They did. Sweet girls. Frightened. I offered to call the police—"

"Why didn't you?"

"Trek," Karma warned.

"Did you lure them in? Did you work for Mara?"

Karma grabbed my arm. "Enough."

The woman blinked, calm despite my voice.

"They were safe when they left," she said softly. "I gave them food. Told them they could rest here anytime."

I scanned the room. **Photos. Artifacts. Objects of another era.** My eyes landed on one photo.

The man.

My stomach coiled.

"Who is that?"

She looked. "Dirk. My mother's lover."

"He looks like Mara."

"I know."

I didn't speak. Just filed it away. Another thread. **Another past bleeding forward.**

Outside, Karma leaned in. "You need to breathe."

"I'm fine."

"You're unraveling."

I looked away. "They're still alive." **Planning Stage: Tactical Reset**

We moved to a nearby rooftop. Neutral space. Noise below, stars above.

"I want to try something," I said. "A rewrite."

Karma blinked. "Of?"

"The wrist devices. Their comms. What if we inject a program —straight into the neural network? **Reboot their muscle memory, mitochondria, DNA.**"

"A mind-body boost?" she said, the wheels already turning. "If we time it right..."

"We can give them what they need."

She nodded, already coding. "Short-term burn. Enough to break restraints, fight, run."

I watched the screen. Watched her. Her hands flying like fire.

"You think it'll work?" I asked.

"I think it has to."

She encoded the burst: cellular enhancement, brain-body sync, temporary surge.

She sent it.

And whispered, "Be ready."

(((((O)))))

FEED ACTIVE. **Nenah. Kaya.**

I felt it before I saw it.

The jolt. The shift in Kaya's spine. The snap of Nenah's breath as power surged through her. The entire feedback feed flared— like adrenaline became code.

They moved.

Fast. Precise. Unnatural.

They were awake.

My heart punched my ribs as I watched Nenah flip an android clean over its back. Kaya grabbed a pipe—bam—right through another's synthetic skull.

Karma's voice cracked with awe. "It's working."

I didn't answer.

Because I was already back in that dust-stained corridor. The one I left him in.

The partner whose breath I can still feel on the side of my neck.

The one who told me: "Push the limits, Trek. No one's coming. Be the rescue."

And then I never saw him again.

(((((O)))))

REALITY CUT BACK IN.

"We should send a telepathic location signal," Karma said.

"No," I snapped. "We can't risk a mental link being intercepted."

"It's a frequency they already share."

"It's reckless."

"It's them."

I paused.

Then gave her a nod.

We sat. Cross-legged. Palms together.

Breath synced. Minds merged.

"Meet in a safe space... at Café Du Monde."

We repeated it again.

Again.

(((((O)))))

SOMEWHERE FAR AWAY, Nenah blinked.

She turned to Kaya.

"We need to go to the temple."

I felt it in my chest. The link landed.

They heard us.

I stood, breath shallow but steady. "We're not losing them again."

Karma's comm pinged.

Director NYX.

"Agent 417. Karma will break off and follow the trail of the missing agents. You continue the retrieval."

She didn't wait for confirmation.

Karma looked at me. "Be careful."

I gave her a small nod. "Bring them home."

We split.

And for the first time in this entire mission, I didn't feel like a watcher.

I felt like the weapon I was trained to be. A badass mofo!

CHAPTER 15
PRANA DAMAGE

THE NIGHT AIR clung to me like static as I bolted down Decatur, the city's pulse thrumming through my boots.

I wasn't running anymore.

I was hunting—every flicker on the tracker, every heartbeat Kaya's biometric ping gave me, it all told me she was close.

Closer than I deserved, after what she'd just been through.

Karma was gone.

Nyx pulled her off the field for a shadow op, left me flying solo with Agents Krix and Uno—M.I.B. types with clean lines and cleaner lies. Didn't matter.

All that mattered was the ping. Kaya was alive. Nenah too.

The Zen Temple showed up on our grid, and my gut said go. No hesitation. We ghosted through the French Quarter, past drunk jazz ghosts and glitchy memories, until we found it.

Incense on the breeze. Peace behind the gate.

Haruto greeted us like we weren't dragging chaos in our wake.

Just bowed with those calm eyes, as if he already knew why we were there. Maybe he did.

"Namaste," he said. "You've arrived just in time for zazen and tea."

I didn't want tea. I wanted answers. But I nodded, followed him into the garden like some broken soldier craving sanctuary.

Krix and Uno scanned the grounds in silence, and I watched Haruto like a riddle I couldn't solve.

When my hand brushed his, it hit me—déjà vu. But deeper. Older. Like we'd fought side by side in another war.

He didn't flinch. Just looked me in the eye and asked, "Do you know someone named Diego?"

The name twisted in my gut. Familiar and foreign. "No," I lied. Or maybe I didn't. Yet.

He nodded once, that same eerie calm.

Before he turned to leave, he paused. **Studied me for a second longer.**

"Would you like to see what I saw?"

There was no fear in his tone—just gravity. I nodded.

Haruto stepped forward, placed his thumb against my temple, and his fingers across my brow—right over my third eye.

And then—Like a glass shattering inward, my senses folded. Light turned viscous. I wasn't in the healing room anymore.

I was squatting beside a man I didn't recognize—Diego?— whispers caught in our throats. We were armed, moving in silence. There was something we had to neutralize. Something not human.

I glanced around and—**Pods. Dozens. Hundreds.**

Transparent suspension cells lined the room—stacked, floating, humming.

Inside: Naked people. Mouths sealed by organic tubes. Ears wired. Eyes forcibly open, blinking with dry panic. Even their limbs—restrained, wired, pulsing with data. **Alien beings floated** beside them, caught in similar stasis. All of them plugged in. Tagged. Cataloged.

My stomach turned. DEXX tried to process the scene but flickered.

❖ DEXX: Biometric feedback corruption. Visual overlay—unstable. Subject identifiers unknown.

Another jolt hit me, and I was pulled deeper—through the wall, into another chamber.

A black room filled with glowing boxes—rectangular towers stacked floor to ceiling. Servers? Data vaults? Machines blinked silently. A low hum vibrated under my skin. No, not hum—chanting. Like the machines were praying.

Toxic. The air here felt artificial, poisonous. My skin buzzed with rejection.

Then I was yanked back—like something inside me refused to stay.

I gasped. My vision steadied just as Haruto pulled his hand away.

He was pale. **Breathing shallow.**

I gripped the edge of Kaya's bed and blinked fast, grounding myself in the soft light of the temple.

"What the hell was that?" I asked.

Haruto steadied himself with one hand against the wall. His voice was low. "A vision. One I didn't seek."

I opened my palm, **fingers twitching.**

❖ DEXX: Internal perception override detected. Cross-link initiated by external source. ❖ Subject: Diego—match: None. Logging fragment for future review.

Haruto looked at me again, his voice calmer now.

"Whatever's coming, it's already seen you."

(((((O)))))

LATER... Enso—the young monk—came to find me. Nenah was asking for me. I sprinted to her faster than I meant to.

When we hugged, the air changed. Felt like pulling someone out of deep space and finding them still breathing. Barely.

But Kaya wasn't with her.

"She collapsed," Nenah said. "Haruto's helping."

I pushed past dread, followed them into the healing chamber —and stopped cold.

The room was glowing.

Kaya lay beneath a lattice of golden thread, her chest rising slow but steady. Haruto stood over her, hands alight like twin suns, whispering ancient mantras I didn't know but somehow understood.

"Did my upgrade do this?" I asked.

Haruto didn't answer at first. He just watched the light thread through Kaya's body, **through her kosha's, those energy sheaths I barely believed in until now.**

"She was already fractured," he said finally. "The program didn't break her. It just lit up the cracks."

I swallowed hard, my pulse syncing with hers.

For a second, I saw the echo of someone else—him …

The last partner I ever let get that close—Field op. Same rhythm. Same slow breath before the leap. His final one.

I blinked it away. **No room for ghosts tonight.**

Kaya stirred. Whispered Haruto's name like a prayer. Then slipped under again. I stayed until her vitals evened out.

(((((O)))))

NEXT MORNING, Haruto invited me to meditate with them. I did. I don't know why.

Maybe to calm the storm in my chest.

Maybe to honor whatever this temple was trying to tell me.

After breakfast, I asked for a war room. Haruto gave us one. **Bare floors. Candlelight. Good enough.**

The agents arrived not long after. We pooled intel, projected the building schematics Karma left me, and still … nothing solid. The map was fog.

Until Uno stepped up with his crystal trick.

Nenah went under easy. Too easy. Like she'd done this in a past life.

"Plaza Tower," she murmured.

The name hit like coordinates to a weapon.

Basement level. Steps. Hell.

We had our lead.

Kaya walked in not long after. Alive. Upright. Stronger than she had any right to be.

Her eyes caught the projection. Confused.

"That's not where I was," she said.

She pointed toward Jackson Square.

Shit.

Two locations. One truth. Or maybe two traps.

And somewhere, Mara was still out there—one step ahead.

I stared at that map, heart racing, one hand on the datapad, the other on instinct.

This isn't over. It's just beginning.

PART THREE
THE INFINITE ODYSSEY

CHAPTER 16
BANG BANG BANG

THE MORNING SUN **slid through** the temple's high celestial windows, casting long, golden streaks across the table.

That table … solid, worn, and sacred. Felt like it had held a thousand conversations, a thousand missions. And now it was holding ours.

We gathered around it, each of us clutching steaming cups of tea, the scent rising between us like silent smoke signals.

No one said it out loud, but we all felt it—today was the day. That sharp focus was written all over their faces.

No fear. Just mission in the bloodstream.

Time to fuck shit up.

The air still held the tail end of Nag Champa incense from an earlier session.

Always grounding.

Always reminding us who we were beneath all the chaos.

I sat at the head of the table, recon data spread out in front of me from Agents Krix and Uno.

With a flick of my wrist, blueprints of the warehouse snapped onto the wall—lines, grids, access points, escape routes.

Cold facts glowing in cool blue.

The others fell into silence, eyes locked in, processing. Nenah zeroed in on the floor plans. I caught her expression—she was somewhere else. Somewhere dark. That place had scarred her. And her brother… still out there.

I felt the shift before I saw it—Haruto moved. Quiet grace, as always.

He walked over to Nenah and sat beside her, his whole vibe **exuding calm like a damn monk battery charger.** She didn't say a word, but I could feel her breathing even out. That's Haruto for you.

"We must move in with swift, covert, decisive action," I said, my voice low but sharp. "Mara won't stay idle once he knows we're on him."

My eyes scanned the blueprints, **mind running the angles like a chessboard.**

"We'll need to split up. Cover more ground. Fast in, fast out."

Haruto leaned in, that gentle tone of his like a ripple across the tension. "My monks, Enso and Ren, are at your disposal. We'll aid you however we can."

His calm was contagious. But the absence across from me hit like a missing tooth.

Kaya's empty seat reminded us all of what this fight cost. What we were risking. What we were willing to sacrifice to finish it.

Agent Uno stepped in next with the warehouse rundown.

Food orders. Guest arrivals. Deliveries that didn't match the manifest.

Patterns that screamed something isn't right. The energy in the room snapped tighter. It was all coming together.

Ideas started firing in my head. Uno's intel.

The floor plan. Entry points. "We need a way in that won't trip alarms. A distraction…" I paused, then grinned. "Food delivery. That might be our ticket."

Didn't take long—Ren and Nenah jumped at the idea. **Willing. Ready.**

But Nenah… damn. She'd already been through enough.

I looked straight at her, my brow tight. "You sure about this?"

She didn't flinch. "I'll do whatever it takes to find my brother."

That hit me in the gut. I nodded. **Respect. Trust. Locked in.**

"Then let's make sure you're prepared," I said, glancing at Haruto. "We'll need a crash course in **your multi-dimensional meditation and martial arts** before we move."

Haruto nodded, that calm assurance never leaving him. "We'll make sure you're ready."

And just like that, the plan clicked into place. Krix and Uno would be stationed at the waterfront side door—backup if shit went sideways. Haruto and Enso? Coming in from above, tactical and unseen.

We trained hard. No bullshit. Haruto and his monks didn't hold back, and we didn't ask them to. Breath synced. Bodies sharpened. Hours flew by in a blur of sweat, focus, and fire.

By evening, I called them back in. One last rundown. "Get some rest. We'll need every ounce of strength come morning. First call is 2:30 a.m.—we review the plan, prep for anything new."

I scanned their faces. Tired, yeah. But ready.

They nodded, filed out, faded into the temple halls.

Lights out.

(((((O)))))

MORNING CRACKED OPEN SLOW, like the calm before a storm.

I was up before the call time, pacing the temple room while the others slept.

Couldn't shake the itch crawling behind my eyes. Had to re-check the plan. Re-check the exits. Re-check everything. Couldn't afford to miss shit. Not today.

I tapped the side of my specs and called up the mission overlay—DEXX humming silently as it filtered ambient scans, team vitals, updated city traffic, and alert triggers from the area grid. I wasn't just reviewing the mission. I was feeling it through a second brain.

❖ DEXX: Nenah—**active**. Reviewing schematics.

❖ DEXX: Haruto + Enso—**meditative state**, temple garden.

❖ DEXX: Krix + Uno—status: awake. **Reviewing supply logs**. No anomalies.

❖ DEXX: Kaya--no active signal.

The absence hit me again. Hard.

She still wasn't here.

I studied the feed until the door finally slid open. Haruto and Enso entered, followed by Kaya.

I let out a breath I didn't know I was holding.

She was back.

Relief hit like a warm current, but my body stayed locked in. No time for softness.

She scanned the wall projection, brow furrowed. I filled her in —Plaza Tower, Nenah's regression, escape patterns, probable layouts. But her frown deepened.

"That's not where I was held," she said. "It was near the river. Jackson Square."

DEXX immediately flagged the discrepancy and overlaid a split-screen comparison.

❖ DEXX: Conflict detected. Subject Kaya – location mismatch. Neural signature consistent. Suggest deeper scan.

Haruto stepped forward, reading the room. "It's possible both are true… or one of them is a manipulated perception. We need clarity."

He turned to Nenah. "With your permission, I'd like to scan you."

She nodded. Haruto scanned her auric field. DEXX chimed in.

❖ DEXX: Foreign signal detected. Subdermal implant — left mastoid region.

Uno moved fast, extracted the device. **A neural disruptor.**

DEXX confirmed it before Uno could finish scanning.

❖ DEXX: Mind scrambler confirmed. Origin: Unknown. Likely Mara tech.

Nenah looked like she'd just opened a door in her own memory and found it bricked over. It was enough to turn our blood cold.

Uno's data feed picked up new movement.

❖ DEXX: Warehouse—riverfront location. Guard patterns increasing. Supply chain anomalies confirmed.

Everything snapped into place.

Time to move.

CHAPTER 17

WHAT IS THIS PLACE?

SNEAKING IN. Nenah and Ren rolled in with the food delivery car, their disguises blending effortlessly into the dim chaos around the warehouse. But that damn black delivery van —the one we'd clocked earlier—was still parked right there.

Too still. Too quiet.

That thing's a ghost just waiting to jump.

The door hung open. Empty. Not good.

They parked beside it and exchanged a glance—silent comms passed through the eyes—then peeled off to the far side of the warehouse.

I was already posted up, cloaking field active, shadows folding around me like armor.

Not a whisper of my presence. **Just intent. Focused. Coiled.**

❖ DEXX: Van status unchanged. Signal trace negative. Nenah + Ren: visual confirmation—approaching east entrance.

Nenah and Ren grabbed the pizzas and slipped into role. Classic low-wage delivery posture—slouched shoulders, distracted eyes, impatient body language. The lab tech barely looked at them. His assistant waved them toward the car without a second thought.

Routine dulls awareness. Makes you blind. That's the advantage.

They returned to the vehicle.

Showtime.

I slipped through the entrance—silent, precise. No hesitation. I was the blade in the dark.

First thing: schematics. I flicked the overlay up—blueprints bathing the edges of my vision, ghosting over the real thing. Exits, blind corners, ventilation choke points—**every pixel had to match.**

I moved fast, checking structures against memory. Each shadow, every flickering bulb, every corner where death could be hiding.

❖ DEXX: Architectural deviations: minimal. Internal grid 94% consistent with mission map.

The skylight loomed above. Kaya, Haruto, and Enso crouched up there, ready. Waiting. The tension between us hummed even through the comm silence.

They feel it too. Something's wrong.

Then I saw them.

The pods.

Rows of them. Eerie, clinical. Too perfect. Just like Kaya and Nenah said—hibernation tech. Some human. Some... definitely not. All of them frozen in that blank between-life space.

What the hell is this place.

I moved closer, jaw tight, breath held. The closer I got, the stronger the pulse of wrong in the air. Something about the layout, the air pressure, the feel of the space—it didn't match the mission brief. The schematics were right.

But the room was... off. Shifted.

❖ DEXX: Electromagnetic field distortion detected. Residual quantum bleed.

"Kaya," I whispered, voice tight, "you got eyes on Mara?"

There was a beat. Then her voice crackled in, sharp.

"I see him. Fourth and fifth row. He's walking between them—real casual. Like he's proud of this mess."

Got him. I nodded, a silent reflex, and pinged the team: Target in sight. Going loud.

I dropped the cloak. Stepped out.

Every move forward was steady, intentional. Mara's back was turned, unaware—or so I thought. **I raised the cuffs.**

He turned. Smiling.

No way. He sensed me. He knew.

His laughter rang out—low, sharp, wrong. His eyes gleamed with something not quite human. **That reptilian glint** I'd seen before in ops that went sideways.

I froze for a half-second, processing.

Shit. He's not alone in there. Something's wired into him.

Above, I felt it before I saw it—movement. Haruto, Kaya, and Enso dropped from the rafters like shadows with weight, weapons at the ready.

Game on.

The warehouse felt alive. Lights flickering like a warning. Steam hissing from unseen vents. The air tasted chemical and stale. And under it all—something thrumming.

Not mechanical. Not quite psychic.

❖ DEXX: Pulse interference: increasing. External comms: intermittent.

In a tucked-away corner, Krix and Uno hit a dead zone. A room that shouldn't exist.

They froze.

"Not on the map," Krix said, voice edged with instinctive fear.

Banks of monitors flickered on. And in the center: a portal gate.

Uno stepped toward the console, fingers twitching over strange glyphs. "Whatever this is—it ain't just travel tech."

His hand slipped. Click.

The door sealed behind them.

Krix cursed. "We're locked in."

At that exact second, deep in the warehouse, something stirred.

Androids. Their systems came online—red eyes flaring like hellfire. One by one, they turned. Sensed us. All of us.

❖ DEXX: Hostile network sync. Multiple nodes activating. Proximity threat: red.

Mara knew.

Of course he did.

I stepped forward, gun raised. "Mara. It's done. You surrender, or we drop this whole place on your head."

He just smiled again.

Chilling. Arrogant.

"You still don't get it, do you?" he said. "You're the small piece, Trek. The blade they send in when they're too scared to face the truth themselves. But you're in my game now."

His voice went cold.

"Tell me—how many of you came?"

Before I could answer, the androids moved.

Fast.

The warehouse exploded into motion. Red-eyed machines fanned out, hunting through the shadows like predators.

Above, Kaya and the others engaged—fluid strikes, zero wasted energy. They fought like they trained for this exact moment. Because we had.

I didn't wait.

Move.

I lunged at Mara—hit him hard, grappled fast. We locked in a flurry of strikes, bone meeting flesh, metal brushing metal. But the bastard was trained.

Dangerous. Smiling through every hit.

He kicked my weapon away—clatter, gone.

Then he ran.

I didn't stop to think.

Run.

I gave chase, up the catwalks, boots pounding steel, **pulse thunderous.**

He ducked into an elevator, fingers dancing across a side panel.

Top floor.

Meanwhile, Kaya, Haruto, and Enso fought back-to-back against the swarm. **Their movements seamless**—Kaya's sharp angles, Haruto's brutal efficiency, Enso flowing like water.

At the top of the catwalk, Mara turned to his scientists—Iyorek and Kael—who'd frozen during the chaos.

"Back to work," he snapped. "I'll handle the intruders."

The deeper we got, **the weirder this place felt.**

It wasn't just a warehouse.

The architecture twisted subtly. Corners curved where they shouldn't. The air had that charge—like standing inside a storm about to drop.

❖ DEXX: **Dimensional flux increasing. Structural variance logged.**

Above, Kaya tried to re-establish comms. The signals were corrupted. Distorted.

Haruto frowned. "This place... it's shifting. Not stable."

Enso added, "It changed when we left the ground floor. Like a maze reacting to us."

Back at the top, Mara reached a control panel. The interface bloomed in front of him—full spatial map. Everyone's position. Tagged. Tracked.

❖ DEXX: Spatial scan breach. Location signatures exposed.

He grinned.

"Got you all," he whispered.

Then **he triggered the portal.**

It roared to life—a swirling mouth of energy, chaos spiraling.

In the control room, Krix and Uno froze as the vortex built pressure, dragging everything toward it.

Seconds. That's all they had.

CHAPTER 18
424

Mara's voice slithered through the air, smug and slow, dripping with the kind of arrogance only a being who thinks he's already won can afford.

"You see, Agent Trek... Earth's been on our radar for quite some time. Even before the 'Trinity' explosions, our probes were monitoring this planet's every move. Eons. You're just catching up."

I clenched my fists.

He was stalling. Trying to get in my head. But I bit anyway.

"Why are you cloning people?"

He smirked. "Why should I tell you anything?"

He paused, staring into me. Not at me—into me. Searching for fear.

Fifteen seconds of silence stretched like wire. Then he tilted his head.

"I may as well tell you. You're in the last stages of your life, after all."

Cute.

"The clones are insurance," he continued. "If any NexaHunt players die, we replace them. **Efficiency. Control. Survival. Dominance.**"

My jaw locked. His words clawed into my brain.

Clones.

Replacements.

Swapping people like gear.

My breath hitched. "Wow. So you've been using Earthlings. Selling them. Playing god... and who knows what else."

He just nodded like I was finally catching up.

"We're not the only ones. Other species have had their fun too. The Anunnaki? They made their kind. **Played with their DNA.** Tried to mold them into the perfect servant—soldier, slave, pawn. This human group are just one of seven other failed attempts."

He stepped closer, voice still silky and cruel.

"When the Anunnaki left during the deluge, all their progress was lost. But then... something else came. Something more advanced. They didn't start over. **They edited. Mutated.**"

What the hell is he even talking about? I didn't know half of this—barely briefed. Had to play like I did.

"They're still experiments, Trek. **Rats in a maze.** You keep trying to crawl out, but the walls shift. We've got pawns in place—politicians, entrepreneurs, media. They don't even know they're disposable. Once the plan activates? They'll be the first to burn."

I tried to keep my voice calm, but it cracked anyway.

"You're violating every contact protocol. This isn't just illegal—its galactic treason."

He laughed.

Didn't even pretend to take me seriously. And all the while, I could feel it—something slithering into my mind. **Subtle. Cold.** Like static crawling across my skull.

No.

❖ DEXX: Deflector frequency modulating. Neural intrusion attempt detected. Mara active on psychic band.

That bastard was inside.

"Don't make me end you," **I growled, heart pounding, blood fizzing with adrenaline.**

But inside? Anxiety curled like smoke. I wasn't sure I could stop him.

The air shifted. Mara's presence receded for a moment—but the damage lingered like a bruise behind my eyes.

DEXX pinged again.

❖ DEXX: Central system shift detected. Energy barrier deployment in 3... 2...

A pulse slammed outward. Walls hardened into light—solid and glowing. Entrances vanished. **Escape points sealed.**

Trapped.

The floor beneath me vibrated. My HUD jittered.

❖ DEXX: Structure is no longer grounded. Magnetic field distortion suggests vertical detachment.

My breath caught.

"Are we lifting off?" I whispered, mostly to myself.

❖ DEXX: Negative. Spatial displacement event likely. Coordinates shifting.

(((((O)))))

❖ DEXX: External team status — Outside, the others regrouped. Kaya, Haruto, Enso, Ren, Nenah—they'd made it out.

I saw their blurred energy signatures.

Tense. Waiting.

The moon behind them looked smaller now. *Off-angle. Wrong.*

❖ DEXX: External team status — escape path secure. Agent 419: biometric return unavailable. Location signature: none.

My stomach dropped.

Wait... what?

I blinked hard, pulled up DEXX's full logs.

❖ DEXX: Alert. Internal Feed 38-A. Timestamp: 00:31. Subject match: Agent 419. Status: restrained. Location: Sublevel Holding Bay.

The image snapped into view.

Karma. Strapped to a slab.

Timestamp: thirty minutes ago.

No.

My chest locked up. I staggered back a step.

She was already inside?

I slammed my comm.

"Director Nyx, this is Trek. Agent 419 and I received your directive to split up. She said you told her to support me in the field—what's your status?"

Static.

Then:

"Trek, I gave no such directive. 419 should be with you."

The world tilted.

She's already in here.

I let her walk into it.

The comm glitched again.

Then Mara's voice returned, smooth and mocking, dragging across my brain like velvet over barbed wire.

"Took you long enough."

DEXX pinged a cascade of red alerts.

❖ DEXX: Portal activation detected. Location: sublevel control chamber.

I ran. Fast. Toward the stairwell. Toward the rising hum.

Down below, Krix and Uno were trapped. I saw them through a flickering live feed—staring down a swirling vortex of energy, the air around them warping like it was being eaten.

The ship—this warehouse—wasn't a building anymore. It was alive. Awake. Shifting between planes.

❖ DEXX: Dimensional bleed confirmed. **Emergency extraction** recommended.

"Working on it," I muttered. "Don't die on me."

The upper deck lights strobed.

Feedback shrieked across open channels.

Console lights blinked in erratic patterns—no rhythm, no logic.

And above it all, Mara.

Fingers on a glowing interface. Watching us scramble like ants in a burning maze.

He looked up. Smiled.

"This is the part where the rats eat each other."

CHAPTER 19
WHERE?

I FINALLY REACHED MARA.

He stood there like he'd been expecting me.

Not afraid. Not surprised.

Just... entertained. Like I was the last lap in some twisted game he'd already won.

He held a weapon in one hand, the other wrapped around Dr. Iyorek's collar, dragging him forward like a rag doll.

"It's over, Mara. Let them go," I barked.

His eyes gleamed—predator sharp. "Do you believe you've won, Agent Trek?"

His laugh grated through me. He nodded, like I was a child who just didn't get it.

"You're just as deluded as ever."

Then, without a flicker of hesitation, he raised his weapon and—

BANG!

Iyorek dropped. Dead. Cold. I shouted, fury ripping out of me like thunder.

"You're INSANE!"

I lunged.

We collided. Fists. Elbows.

Rolling across the catwalk, each trying to gain control. He was fast. Unnaturally fast. **Long limbs wrapped around me—inhuman.** His hand clamped around my throat, legs locking mine down like a goddamn spider.

Then I saw it—his face. It was changing.

Morphing.

One second Mara.

Next second... a Grey.

No. Two beings. One body.

What the hell ARE you?

I triggered a DNA scan. It confirmed what my instincts already knew—symbiotic. **Two separate organisms** fused as one.

Shit.

That's when it hit me.

A wave of... nothing.

Defeat.

Submission.

Hopelessness.

No. That's not me. That's not who I am.

I roared and threw everything I had into one strike, breaking his hold. He hissed, sprang off me like a creature with too many joints, and disappeared—cloaked.

I didn't hesitate.

Eye implant—switch to infrared.

There. Crawling up the wall. Spider-like.

And that's when the static started.

They came out of the walls. Greys. Flickering like bad reception, slipping between dimensions. Surrounding me.

They moved like they were glitching—unreal.

Then I felt it. Them. In my mind.

They pushed. Tried to rewrite me. I gritted my teeth. My implant kicked into overdrive, blocking what it could. But it wasn't enough.

My knees buckled.

Then I saw them—

Ants. Thousands of them. Crawling up my legs, inside my suit, inside my skin. I screamed, swatting, staggering.

"It's not real."

Haruto's voice.

Not from a comm.

Inside me.

His ethereal form shimmered just out of sight, drifting around me like a ghost of clarity.

"It's a mind assault. Shift your thoughts. Now."

I focused.

The ants bloomed.

Flowers.

Falling off me in waves of color and light.

The Greys staggered. Confused.

Then they came again.

(((((O)))))

OUTSIDE, **VIA DEXX's technology**, my implants continued updating me. Haruto, Enso, and Ren sat in a triangle—knees touching, eyes closed, bodies humming with psychic force.

Between them, a glowing orb swirled.

A barrier. A tether. My last line of defense.

DEXX monitored everything. **Real-time overlays. Signal degradation.** Threat level red.

Kaya stood watch—blade ready, eyes on the warehouse. No blink. No breath wasted.

The space around the structure warped.

DEXX pinged urgently.

❖ DEXX: Internal signature match. Feed 38-B activated. Subject: Trek. Status: Neural breach attempt ongoing. Hostile entities detected.

❖ DEXX: Deploying temporary override. Initiating defense protocol: Counter-intrusion.

The Greys came one by one, testing me. Like they were studying me. Every strike I landed, they adapted. Every thought I had, they tried to twist.

Haruto held them off—barely. His mind linked with mine, fighting like a shield around my consciousness.

But our connection wavered.

Too much interference. Too many variables.

He released me before he got locked out.

That's when I saw it.

A pod in the corner. Labeled "424."

Inside—Nano. Nenah's brother.

My heart stopped.

He was pale. Still. Suspended.

But alive.

No time.

I pulled the smart bomb from my wrist, tapped the release code, and dropped it into the center of the floor.

A pulse exploded outward—blue static shockwave—targeted to spare anything with my DNA.

The Greys reeled.

I charged, shattered the control panel, and ripped open the pod.

Nano's body fell into my arms like dead weight.

Please don't be dead.

I slung him over my shoulder, **sprinting.**

Behind me, Mara reappeared, face warping again.

He activated a portal.

"You're such an inconvenience," he sneered. "But this isn't over."

He vanished into the void. Coward.

I ran.

The ship was destabilizing—walls flickering, architecture shifting.

I activated the portable portal on my belt.

The vortex shimmered open.

I stepped through—

But just as I crossed the threshold, **a Grey grabbed my leg.**

BOOM!

A violent explosion rocked the entire ship.

(((((O)))))

SMOKE CURLED AROUND ME.

Voices — broken, distant, like sound underwater.

Kaya. Ren. Enso.

❖ DEXX: *Signal disruption. Tracking lost. Trek vital signs: unknown. Nano status: unknown.*

I tightened my grip around him — Nano — 424.

Couldn't feel my fingers anymore. **Could barely feel the kid's weight against my chest.**

Hold on, damn it. Just hold on.

The warehouse shuddered — then twisted sideways, like reality itself slipped a gear.

A sonic boom cracked the levee behind us.

Heat smashed into me. **Fire blossomed from nowhere**, swallowing the perimeter, shredding steel and concrete.

Sirens screamed through the smoke — distant, useless.

❖ DEXX: *Attempting uplink to Nyx command node... No response.*

Kaya's voice — raw and razor-edged — punched through the chaos:

"DEXX, confirm—Trek made it through the portal?"

Silence.

Then —

❖ DEXX: *Portal signature logged. Exit point: unstable. Cross-dimensional drift detected.*

My chest seized.

My body — just static now, just scatter.

Kaya's voice sliced back in:

"Keep scanning. Don't stop until you find him."

No.

Find us.

I tried to answer. Tried to move.

But the world was already collapsing inward — colors, sounds, faces melting into static.

Memories blinked out like dying stars.

All that remained was the grip around Nano.

The one thing I refused to let go of.

This isn't the end.

Not even close.

Then the universe cracked — and we were gone.

ACKNOWLEDGEMENTS

I want to acknowledge my mom, Mirtha and dad, Carlos, whose boundless love and progressive wisdom have shaped me into who I am today. Open-minded, determined, and respectful. Your guidance and encouragement have been the foundation of my success, and I am forever indebted to you.

To my aunt Ruth, who named me and who, like my parents, was instrumental in her way, "challenge everything that makes no sense." Sadly, she passed away before this book was published.

I want to acknowledge my beloved siblings, nieces and nephews, aunts and uncles for their support throughout my book writing journey. They have been the most open-minded, strong beings anyone can ask for. I am eternally grateful to have y'all in my life.

To my awesome adopted family, my book club peeps, my sisters from another mother and planet, y'all know who you are. Y'all have been my rocks at various times along our shared timeline, standing by me through thick and thin.

Your unwavering encouragement and inspiration have been the fuel that kept me going. Your friendship has enriched me and transformed my life in ways I cannot express.

This book is dedicated to all of you, my family, friends, and parents, for your belief in me. Thank you for being the pillars of strength in my life.

I almost forgot to mention who got me my first writing tablet.
Jimmy, thank you so much for believing in me enough to give
me something to write my ideas on while working.

Love Copper

THANK YOU

I have to mention the places that inspired me to write. A very special thank you to providing the place and vibe.

Cured on Columbia

Southern Hotel

Haven

Black Flower Records

ABOUT THE AUTHOR

Copper Wiezi is an emerging author of sci-fi-themed fantasy. This is his first published book.

For more information please visit www.copperwiezi.com

facebook.com/copperwiezi
x.com/CopperWiezi
instagram.com/copperwiezi

ALSO BY COPPER WIEZI

In the Dario Trek Series

Book 1 NexaHunt

Pre Order Now!

Book 2 Beta Frequency

Other books in the works:

Divine Hack

DEPLOYED